ALSO BY
DONNA WELCH JONES

Sheriff Lexie Wolfe Novels

Killing the Secret

Deadly Search

Terror's Grip

Murder & Beyond

Deranged Justice

Anthologies

"Come Die with Me" in *A River of Stories*

"Old Guys and Dead People" in *Shades of Tulsa*

UNBREAK THEIR HEARTS

BY

DONNA WELCH JONES

Twisted Plot Publishing

DEDICATION

To the women who have put their broken lives back together
And those who continue to live in fear

NEVER FORGET
You are valuable
You are deserving
You are strong

* * * * *

The National Domestic Violence Hotline

1-800-799-SAFE (7233)
1-800-787-3224 (TTY)

* * * * *

ACKNOWLEDGMENTS

Thank you to the following individuals:

Detective Brian Gerber, Myrna Ellingson Kurle,
Shirley Corwin, Dr. Karen Cornell, Bill Wetterman

Mark H. Jones, Licensed Marriage & Family Therapist and
Licensed Professional Counselor

Sarah Henning, Nikki Hanna, Damonza Cover Design

Dana Delamar, By Your Side Self-Publishing

CHAPTER ONE

THE BEAST

"Don't be a fool, Marcy. You'll never get rid of boss man if you start dating him."

"It's not dating," I snapped. "He's a good guy... lonely."

"Or he's a lecher, who manipulated to get you alone."

I aimed a throw pillow at Von's head, unfortunately missing his smug face. "Theo's forty-four, twice my age. I'm like his daughter. Anyway, you don't like him because he's homophobic."

"One of several reasons my creep detector goes to high when he's around."

"I told Theo his employees would accuse him of favoritism. Didn't think my best friend would be the first to get jealous."

"It's not about jealousy. It's about protecting my favorite person—you. What if he wants a lover instead of a pretend daughter?"

"If it gets uncomfortable, which it won't, I'll think of something. I can't lose my job."

Von's hands gripped the arms of his chair. "He threatened your job?"

"Mentioned that he fired four people last week."

"We've got to get you out of this."

"Too late. He told me to arrive at 8 p.m. tonight. Promised me a fabulous dinner." I wrapped a strand of blond hair around my finger, and waited for outrage.

"MARCY, NO!"

"It's just dinner."

Von's features clenched. "Then what?"

"Give me a break. I live from paycheck to paycheck—I can't afford to insult him."

"I guess you'll become an essential employee if he screws you."

I slammed my Coke can on the glass-topped table. "LEAVE, I need to get dressed."

"Phone when you get home," he ordered.

I didn't respond, but glared as he stood and shook his head before slamming out my apartment door.

I slipped a modest black sheath over my head, and put on a silver jacket. I combed my hair into a slick ponytail, then wrapped it into a knot at the base of my neck. A strand of fake pearls added to my classy conservative appearance, I hoped.

No backup plan sprang from my brain as I drove my red Mustang to Theo's house.

"Calm down girl," I reprimanded myself. "You're getting upset over nothing." Theo's a nice man not a serial killer. Von, not logic, put these sinister thoughts in my head.

White stone with navy shutters adorned Theo's mansion. A stained glass ocean scene replaced the front picture window. The doorbell stuck out from the middle of a huge ship's wheel that dominated the front door. I pressed the bell. The sound of a ship's horn rang.

Theo opened the door wide. His military haircut called attention to his prominent forehead, his clothes a blur of whiteness from shirt to shoes. His face pinched as he spoke, "I see you ignored my request to choose your dinner apparel."

"Feel more comfortable in my own clothes. Anyway, you don't know my size."

"His eyes scanned my body. Size 8 I'd say with a 38D bust, five-foot-five, and 115 pounds. How did I do?"

I nodded as discomfort crept up my spine.

"Come in. Not to worry. No need to change twice. That black dress is adequate for dinner apparel."

2

What did that change twice thing mean?

Theo curved his arm under my elbow, and escorted me into the dining room. One wall displayed a huge aquarium. The words "fish food" streaked across my frayed mind.

He pulled out my chair, then served small plates of tuna bruschetta.

"You're the waiter?"

"Yes, Nella cooked the meal. I sent her home. I can handle everything by myself." He winked, with a half-smile.

I took a bite of appetizer to avoid a comment. It tasted so delightful that I generally would've shrieked. This time, however, churning dread inside my gut took over.

Theo excused himself to the kitchen. Thanks to Von's dark foreboding my brain searched for an escape plan.

Theo returned with grilled swordfish on a bed of white rice. A small salad of mixed veggies occupied a boat-shaped bowl.

"I opened a thirty-year-old bottle of white wine for our special evening." He held it up like a prized trophy.

I slowly shook my head. "You shouldn't have Mr. Lisbon."

His nostrils puffed. "You're very formal, Marcy."

My hands flailed as I spoke. "I'm uncomfortable, sir. I shouldn't be here. The other employees will chastise me."

Words bellowed from his pocked face. "DAMN THEM! They have no business disrupting my personal life."

I managed to whisper. "What about my life?"

He reached out and petted my hair. "I'll take care of you, sweetheart."

My adrenaline spiked. "I don't need taken care of."

"Yes, my pet, you do. I'm the man, who can make your dreams come true."

The soft, threatening caress of his voice popped hairs up on my arms.

"Come," he stood. "I'm too excited to eat dessert."

My heartbeat escalated. "I... I thought you invited me here to get to know me better, like a friend or a daughter."

Anger seeped into his words. "I'm a man, and you're a beautiful young woman. I've wanted you in my bed for months. You're sexy and confident at work. Now you're going to play naiveté?"

"I just talked to you. It meant nothing."

"I picked up on your sexual vibes," he gibed.

He pulled me toward the stairs a vice grip on my hand.

"Sexual harassment is against the policy of your company. Please let me go home."

"You'll leave when I'm satisfied. By the way, I didn't miss your veiled threat."

My brain raced. Even if I snatched my purse from the dining room, no way could I get the keys, and out the door fast enough. I could push him down the steps or crash a vase into his head. Not a good idea to attack the man who signs my checks.

He paused outside an upstairs door. His grip loosened. "What's wrong Marcy? You're acting like a blubbering child."

A wave of nausea forced my hand against the wall for support.

Theo opened the door. "Your outfit is on the bed. I'll get dressed, and be back soon."

The door shut, and the ominous turning of the outside lock skyrocketed my trepidation.

A pile of fur covered one corner of the bed. I lifted it with both hands. Long white fur composed the hood. Two small ears, with pink satin linings, stuck out from the headgear. When worn the attached piece looked like a fur swimsuit without a butt covering. A long white tail hung from the waist past my bare butt, covering my crack. I couldn't face my humiliation in the mirror.

The door swung open. Theo the dog crawled into the bedroom.

"Woof, woof," he barked.

My body stiffened at the edge of the bed.

A clinched-mouth order sizzled out. "Meow. You're my kitten. Play the game if you want a job."

He grabbed an ankle, and pulled me off the bed. He barked. I meowed.

My knees scraped the floor as I raced away. His growl became more and more ferocious as he followed. He nipped at my ass then clawed my thigh as he forced me to my back.

I scratched at his back and reached for his face.

He bent my fingers back. "Not my face, you little fool. Meow like you're fighting for your life."

"Meow, meow, meow," I wailed.

He forced me to the end of the bed. He yipped and yipped as his penis stabbed my anus. One long growl then his body released mine.

My feet plastered to the floor. My face sunk forward into the comforter. The door closed. My brain told me to hurry but my body ached. I rolled to standing. Small bits of blood oozed from bites on my thighs. I reached back and touched my rear. Specks of fresh blood dotted my palm.

I slid the black dress over my head and grabbed my necklace. I missed every other step as I ran down the stairs. I snatched my purse and headed to the door.

I stopped. There he stood, in front of the door, a twisted smile on his face.

"Marcy, I've had such a pleasant evening. However, I didn't appreciate your naiveté. Your uncooperativeness hurt my feelings."

I shivered.

"If you divulge the activities of this evening you'll be roadkill in one way or another."

I nodded.

He held the door open. "Have a pleasant Sunday, Marcy."

I trotted to my car. My hand rummaged in my purse. Panic tightened my chest. *Where are my keys? Did he take them so I'd go back in his house?*

I threw my wallet, Kleenex and lipstick to the passenger side floor. I pressed my hand against the purse lining. My chest rose and fell. I'd have to face the monster again.

One more time, I felt—there, zipped in the side pocket. I shook the key into the ignition, and the engine let out a roar. Placing my bare foot against the etched gas pedal—I didn't realize until right then that my shoes were still upstairs. The bra purposely left—too time consuming.

Tears tracked down my cheeks, and dropped from my chin.

CHAPTER TWO

SAD SUNDAY

Darkness surrounded me even as glimmers of sun danced through my bedroom window.

I lay in the indentation of my ancient mattress trying to focus on the day ahead rather than the night before.

I threw back the cover and examined my legs. Bruises blotted my thighs and one bruised circle ached deeply in my belly where Theo's teeth managed to catch hold.

Obviously an experienced dog man, he left marks that people generally covered with clothes. My hand gently massaged the back of my neck. I'd forgotten the clench of his teeth as he pretended to carry me off.

Slowly I swung my legs around, and sat on the bed's edge. I needed to leave this room of worn furniture and dreary drapes. Perhaps my new living room décor would cheer me.

I cautiously lifted from my bed, and waddled to the bathroom. The floor length mirror reflected a patch of dried blood that curved down my leg from my black and blue ass.

Nausea rumbled inside my stomach as I sank to the floor. The smell of rotted fish polluted the bathroom air as the remains of my dinner sprayed into the toilet.

A few minutes later I grasped the side of the sink to pull myself to standing. The face I saw in the mirror was a broken stranger. *Where had I gone? Why did I let this happen?*

The warm shower gently sprinkled my body as it had at midnight, 2 a.m., and now five hours later. No amount of scrubbing washed the rape from my mind or body.

Old gray jogging pants, and a T-shirt kept my sores from being assaulted by tightness.

The phone rang, rang again, and yet again.

I pulled a chair to the picture window, and watched the rain splatter on the sidewalk below. I closed my eyes to absorb the sounds of random splashes, then watched as the rain danced against the umbrellas as people hurried along the sidewalk. *The angels must be crying for me.*

The phone buzz perpetuated. I wasn't ready for Theo or Von. Likely Theo was phoning to threaten me again. Finally, I looked at the caller ID—Von—then ignored it.

I sat down at the computer, and typed *people who dress like animals during sex* into the search engine. They're called Furries. Never heard of them before, but estimated to be thousands in the U.S. Those turned on by the sexual component are interested in sex with people dressed like animals not real animals.

No underlying mental health issues, according to the Internet. I had the misfortune to come in contact with a perverted exception.

Polite knocks on my door turned to pounding. My body stiffened, my stomach cramped. Dead fish breath huffed from my mouth. Panic froze me. "He'll go away soon," I whispered. "I must not move."

"MARCY," Von bellowed. "Open up or I'm calling the police."

A stiff gait got me to the door. "Hush Von, you're causing a scene."

My neighbor poked her head out, then slammed her door when she saw Von.

His generally fluffy hair was flat as a pancake. Damp auburn strands touched his shoulders. Sweat and or rain soaked his shirtfront.

"What the hell's going on?" He panted as he entered the

room. "I thought Theo took you hostage. You were supposed to call. Did you spend the night with him?"

I left Von dripping on the kitchen floor, and hobbled to get a bath towel and shirt. "Take these, you look like a drowned goose. Von stripped, then dried his flesh. Lastly, he stuck his head through the hole of the old sweatshirt I handed him.

He grinned, "No pink panties to wear?"

"No offense, but I think your rear is a little bigger than mine."

"None taken. Let me point out the sweatshirt is plenty loose."

I placated, "Tall and thin you have a model's body."

"You can't avoid talking about last night, Marcy."

"Can I tempt you with a day old donut?"

"Distraction isn't going to work."

He followed me to the sofa. I pulled the blanket to my waist, and Von cuddled in the other half.

"Tell me."

I chewed on a fingernail. "A real animal."

"Is that why you're walking like a bowlegged cowboy?"

"Had a fall, and landed on my butt."

"You're a lousy liar. Spill your guts."

"Theo's house was nautically themed. He wore a white captain's hat at dinner. Food all had a fish theme."

"Chef there?"

"Theo served the prepared meal."

Von shook his head. "Bad sign that he arranged to get you alone."

"Freaked me out."

Von turned his somber eyes toward me. "After dinner?"

My hands tugged at the blanket edge, "Sex."

"You had intercourse with that scum?"

"He didn't offer another option."

Von squeezed my shoulder. "That bastard."

Sobs wrenched from my mouth. I laid my head on his blanketed lap.

Von wrapped his slender arms around me and patted my back. "He raped you?"

My breath caught as my chest heaved up and down. One word struggled out, "Brutal."

A few minutes later Von released his hold as I slowly calmed.

I wobbled to the counter, and poured grape juice into mugs. The cup wavered as I handed it toward him. He steadied my hand and patted the cushion beside him.

I sat sipping and whimpering, emotionally spent.

"Something needs to be done about that monster, Marcy."

"You warned me. I should've listened."

"Don't give the rapist any slack."

One drip of juice slipped down the side of Von's mug. I watched the drop soak into my new sofa.

Von leaned toward me. "There's more isn't there?"

"I don't want to talk about it ever again. Now Theo won't fire me. That's all that matters."

"I'LL MAKE HIM PAY!"

I squeezed his hand. "Stay out of this Von. Please, for me."

CHAPTER THREE

CRASH AND BURN

Monday morning I searched the back of my closet for a cowl-necked white top to wear to work. Small pearls replaced dangling earrings.

My concealer didn't cover the dark circles under my eyes as well as the commercial promised. Strands of unwashed hair refused to stay in place.

I threw the pillow I was using as my butt cushion in the closet. It would prompt a series of obscene jokes and gossip at work—better to sit and suffer. Yesterday evening I practiced walking, but I still had a hitch in my movement. Hurt to sit and hurt to walk—the only alternative to fly. But at that moment, I felt like an unlikely candidate for the angelic form of movement.

As soon as I passed through the double glass door of the office building I spied Gretta and Megan huddled in the corner. Their frantic words overlapped. That is... until they saw me.

They couldn't know about Theo and me, at least not yet. No different than they usually are—mean.

I quickly turned and headed for the elevator. Gretta's dulled yell stopped me. "Marcy"

Not like her to speak.

They followed me into the elevator—trapped.

"Something going on ladies?" I asked.

"I'll say," Megan's words spit out. "You walked right past the notification."

"What notification?"

"Dillard posted a meeting at 4:30 p.m. for all secretarial staff," Megan's tone fluctuated up and down.

"So?"

Gretta jeered, "You add a new low to dumb blond jokes. That's what happened when Lisbon had Dillard, his executive henchman, lay off four people in janitorial. Called everyone together then axed the poor suckers in front of the group. Twenty-five percent of the staff."

"Humiliating," Megan scoffed. "You'd think he'd have enough dignity to fire them privately."

Gretta chimed in, "He doesn't call it firing. He manipulates the system to avoid paying unemployment."

The elevator stopped on the tenth floor. I shouldered past Gretta toward my office.

Her hurried steps quickly caught up. "You've got nothing to worry about, boss's pet."

I gasped, and squeezed my purse against my belly.

Gretta continued her verbal deluge. Apparently, she'd missed my visceral reaction to her "boss's pet" comment.

"You need to send up a prayer for your boy, Von. I'd bet a hundred that he's fired before the day ends."

I didn't respond. For a second, I wondered why she wasn't more worried about herself. But I knew why. She's worked for Theo's company at least five years. If axed, she'd get unemployment. Von and I received training in the same group ten months ago. As probationary employees, we could be fired without justification. Saturday night was my job security.

Von lived check-to-check—just like me. Both of us, apparently, missed the thrift lessons in elementary school. For once I agreed with Gretta, Von's chance of staying was almost nonexistent. My sofa could turn into his bed, my place into his place. Somehow I'd help him pull through—though his emotional impact would be hard to fix.

The day dragged. The vending machine supplied my unhealthy lunch. I hadn't seen Von all day. Usually, he showed up at noon, but probably didn't want company on the day his world might collapse.

Few people needed to be greeted or pampered at my desk. Of the people I did see, no one shared a smile. Even the employees who were probably safe couldn't be sure—wondering how they'd pay rent or feed their children.

At 4:28 p.m., I walked into the conference room. I slid into a seat beside Von, and held his hand beneath the cover of the table.

Twenty of us sat around the long oval table, which was generally reserved for top executives and clients. Mr. Dillard ominously sat at the head. The creases on his face formed a map of malice.

The Hunger Games cropped up in my brain. Jobs were about to die, and probably lives as people knew them.

Dillard tightened his tie, and cleared his throat. "As you all know our sales are in a pit that grows deeper each day. In order for Theodore Lisbon's company to survive it's necessary to eliminate costs. Our best road to that end is to cut staff. Theo mandated that I terminate twenty-five percent of the staff in each department. That means five members of the clerical staff will be leaving today. I appreciate your contributions to the company. Your dismissals are a necessary part of saving the jobs of your coworkers."

Dillard unfolded a sheet of paper, cleared his throat twice and read in a booming voice. "Von Sandburg." Tears quickly overflowed his eyes.

"Paula Bacone." A stunned expression.

"Lindsey Edwards." A stifled screech disturbed the deadly quiet.

"Megan Barrett." A harsh whisper aimed toward Gretta. "You said I'd be safe."

Gretta did a slow headshake obviously embarrassed for being called out publicly on her promise to Megan.

Dillard's eyes went back to the list. "Final dismissal is Marcy Simon." I froze, unbelieving.

"Goodbye and good luck to each of you," Dillard said. "Leave your name tags. Pick up any personal belongings at your desks before you leave today."

Von ran out the door his sobs trailing down the hall. The

rest of the group cleared silently. I hung back. A couple of women met my eyes with pity. I saw a section of the pattern in Gretta's skirt. She hovered outside the door. Waiting for an earful to spread. Not that she could hear much as Megan hammered her with a stream of cuss words.

Dillard and I were the only two left.

He looked up from gathering his papers. "What do you want, Marcy?"

My voice crackled, "This is a mistake. Theo wouldn't fire me."

"He approved my list. He's known for a week."

"Call him. He wouldn't fire me."

His words punctured the air. "Because you screwed him?"

"I... I can't lose my job."

"Well you have. Theo warned me you'd go berserk."

"I've always done good work," I spouted.

"Get real, Marcy," he sneered. "You're a pretty face with a firm ass and big boobs. That's why Theo hired you. This company can no longer afford the luxury of your special talents. No amount of griping is getting your job back, so shut up and get out."

I ripped the nameplate from my blouse, and threw toward his face. A tiny dot of blood peeked from his cheek where the pinpoint collided with his face.

He pounded the tabletop. "Get out before I call security."

I barged into the hall, the door slamming into Gretta as I tried to plow through.

"Watch out," she huffed.

"I gave the door an extra push. "Get out of my way, you nosey witch!"

I saw no one, nothing, as I threw the personal contents of my desk drawer into the garbage can. Christy came to exchange my last check for my office key. "I'm sorry," she squeaked. I turned away from the hug she was about to deliver, suppressing the urge to run down the hall. Most of the surviving workers surrounded Paula, who screamed about the necessity of moving back in with her overbearing parents. I made it to my car without having to endure the pity of any of the blessedly employed.

I lay across the Mustang's back seat, hoping no one would

see. I didn't want my presence to pique curiosity. Worse still for someone to stop and spout sympathy. I had to confront my rapist.

No peering eyes reached me. At 5:30 p.m. I sat straight, and visually surveyed the near empty parking lot.

Theo's long Lincoln remained parked in the place of honor. He usually left late or early. Likely didn't want to mingle with the riff-raff, and now the newly unemployed.

But there he was. He looked neither left nor right as he walked toward his car. The sneer on his face locked in place. His eyes widened as I positioned myself directly in his line of vision walking forward.

He started to circle me. I sidestepped to the left, and collided into his chest.

"Shit, Marcy. Are you drunk?"

"Dillard fired me today."

"He's my manager. I don't interfere with his decisions." Theo's lips pursed into a sickening smile. "Although, it was a logical move."

I grabbed his shirt. "I can ruin you, pervert."

"You could try, kitten. But everyone would say your accusations were retaliation for being fired. You yourself said I shouldn't play favorites."

My words flamed toward his face. "At the least, DOG, it'd be embarrassing."

"If you ever want another job in this town reconsider your threats. No one I know would hire a vengeful bitch."

"You promised I'd keep my job."

"Not really—you imagined what you wanted to hear. Thought your sweet derriere saved you. Probably surprised it didn't. You've got the looks, but not the action."

"Certainly don't have your sick style."

His hand pushed me aside, and he semi-marched to his vehicle.

I ran to the Mustang. The engine revved in the empty garage as Theo pulled out. *Should've run him over when I had the chance.*

I kept close as he maneuvered down toward the exit. On the slope the Mustang's front nearly touched the Lincoln. His eyes peered into the rear view mirror. My car rammed into the Lincoln's bumper when it reached the exit.

He jumped from his car, rage bursting from his lips. "Crazy bitch. I'll have you locked up."

I struggled out of my car. His mouth hung open as I pulled down my slacks and panties. I turned my black-and-blue ass toward him, then swiveled to reveal my bruised belly and thighs.

"Call the police, demon. I'd be happy to show them your handiwork."

He closed the gap between us and squeezed my chin. "Back off or I'll fry your life." The threatening hand dropped suddenly. His glare strayed from my face.

"What's going on Mr. Lisbon?" The security guard's voice came from behind me.

"This woman has gone lunatic over being fired."

"I'll take care of it, sir, you go home and relax." Gus's tone sounded even, calm.

"That I will." Theo opened his car door then turned back and winked.

I felt embarrassment flush my face as I pulled up my pants.

Gus turned his gaze to the pavement.

"Do you want me to call the police, Marcy?"

I stammered, "To lock me up?"

Gus's voice was gentle. "To call on Theo. I see he hurt you."

His sympathy filled my eyes with tears. Gus fidgeted, obviously unsure of how to comfort me.

I managed to utter a few words. "Boss man has the winning hand. We'd both be destroyed."

His eyes peeked out from caterpillar brows. "Whatever you want. I don't like him to get away with shit."

Gus opened the car door and lifted his hand in farewell.

I started my car, the Mustang engine-revving fine—just a dented front bumper.

———— • ————

Minutes later, soreness slowed my ascent on the apartment stairs. As I rounded the corner, my eyes focused on a figure crumbled against the door a bottle of liquor in his hands.

"Von let me help." I set aside the bottle and pulled him to his feet. Slits of eyes peeked out from a swollen face. He leaned against me as we struggled in the door.

"Come to the bedroom," I directed. A double motive, didn't want him throwing up on my new furniture—soon gone. I stuffed pillows behind him as he reclined on the bed.

"That must be a world's record for getting drunk. You've only been off work a couple of hours."

"Lots of motivation," Von took a gulp from the booze bottle he continued to grasp as if a life preserver.

My voice quivered, "I understand."

In the kitchen, I prepared coffee and toast before returning to set a tray on the bed beside Von. Fluffing two more pillows, I crawled in bed beside him. We reclined as we sipped coffee and crunched toast for five minutes without words.

Anguish distorted his face. "What are we going to do, Marcy?"

"I haven't a clue."

Our intertwined whimpers grew to sobs. Neither of us attempted to control our tears—there were too many.

CHAPTER FOUR

THE FOUR Fs

Over the next five weeks I applied at every office in the surrounding area. They all said versions of the same thing. "No openings, and none anytime soon." I wondered if Theo sent out a memo not to hire me.

Today I followed my usual Saturday morning routine. Stuck my clothes in the washing machine at the downstairs laundry then up a floor to exercise.

The smell of Old Spice greeted me as I entered the workout room. Samuel, a wiry fellow with thick white hair, ran on the treadmill. He and I were the only two residents stupid enough to exercise at 7 a.m. on a Saturday morning.

The straightness of his carriage, and the firmness of his speech reminded me of Dad.

His thick voice barely carried over the hum of the machine. "I been wondering how much older I am than you."

"I turned twenty-two last month."

Samuel turned off the machine and headed for the weights. "Makes me feel mighty old. Been forty years since I was that age."

"You seem younger. How are you feeling?"

"Pretty good. Have some memory lapses from time to

time. Mostly going fine, but a few miles an hour slower."

"Occasionally, I have the same issue."

Samuel's tone turned serious. "That jerk, Fred, who lives a couple of doors from you thinks you're the prettiest creature he's ever seen."

"Is Fred the man who owns storage units? He seems nice."

Samuel scowled, "That's the guy and he's a pervert. Best keep your distance. If he gets near you throw a chair at him and run the other direction."

Samuel returned twenty-pound weights to the shelf and headed toward the exit.

"Thanks for the warning," I muttered.

His pointer finger flapped toward me. "I'm serious."

I nodded as I continued my triceps extensions.

Next I mounted the treadmill with memories of my father pacing my movement. Samuel's protectiveness likely activated the thoughts in my head.

What would Dad think of Theo getting away with rape? Not difficult to figure out. A quivering bottom lip, a stone face, and daggers shooting from his eyes. "Fight for yourself," he'd say. "Don't let a man degrade you."

History is why I'm so sure of what he'd say. I was fourteen that day in September. Dad came home early from the factory—something he never did. I suspect the nosy neighbor ratted on me.

At the time, Derik was the love of my life—all fourteen years of it. Derik was seventeen and the senior wrestling star—short and stout. My hand caressed his bicep and squeezed. I ran my fingers through the sparse hairs on his barrel chest. He was proud to show me his penis, also short and stout.

Took him five minutes to release my boobs from their protective covering. His touch was clumsy, rough. Derik was pulling down my jean shorts when the front door slammed open hard enough to embed the doorknob into the wall.

Dad's stone face focused on quivering Derik. "Get out boy."

Derik tugged at his jeans to cover up his shrunken manhood, grabbed his shirt, and rounded to the far side of Dad to slip out behind him. Clutching the waist of his pants he bolted out the door.

I stood, silent. My shorts twisted to the right. Two top buttons missed as I hurried to cover my boobs. The air between us was suffocating.

Dad didn't speak.

My words embedded with whimpers. "I love him, Daddy. He said I'd make him the world's happiest guy. He loves me so much."

"Go straighten yourself while I put on supper."

Soon the yelling begins. I'm such a disappointment.

A dinner of leftover stew and cornbread, then he pointed to the sofa. He pulled the old wood rocker a foot in front of me.

My hands gripped each other as I waited for my sentencing.

"You ain't had a mom to tell you things, and I ain't equipped for girl talk. I do know something and that's about teenage boys, because I was one."

Didn't know what to say as he stared into my eyes, so I remained silent.

"Teenage boys want sex. They can't help it just how they're made. Biology says they need to reproduce so they go searching for girls to give them pleasure. When I was a boy we had a motto called the Four Fs: find 'em, fool 'em, fuck 'em and forget 'em."

I felt my face emblazon.

"Never forget that motto when some young guy says he's got to have you. What he's got to have is his penis pumped."

I sank further into the sofa.

"Tell him your dad will shoot him or you're having a period—whatever—just get away from him. You'll end up pregnant, and he'll end up finding another vagina or six or ten to satisfy his urges."

My demeanor shriveled. I studied the floor.

"You're even prettier than your mama. The same blond hair and blue eyes as her, and a smile that lights up this old man's life. Because you're beautiful the boys will brag they bedded you. Your reputation will be ruined. Be proud of the woman you're becoming. Don't give yourself to some sex crazed teenager who'd say anything to get in your pants."

My eyes flickered from side to side, never reaching his face.

"Do you hear what I'm saying, Marcy?"

"Yes, sir."

A drill sergeant tone barked out his mouth, "Tell me."

My words came out so quickly they squished together. "Boys will find me, fool me, f… me, and forget me if I don't respect myself enough to tell them 'no.'"

"Correct." Dad's voice lowered, "As they get older most of them change from sex mongers to good men. You need to wait for one of those guys."

"Yes, Daddy."

I remember how resolute I felt as I promised to keep teen boys out of my vagina. He never spoke of the four Fs again, and I sure didn't.

I hugged him later that night. Even at fourteen I realized how tough it was to have the sole responsibility of raising a daughter. Mom's death choked the joy out of him. Duty to his only child kept him going.

What would Dad think about Theo getting away with rape? Nothing, because he died. Left me alone. A heart attack took Dad two years ago. Quick and dirty, a knife plunged into my life that left me without a family.

CHAPTER FIVE

FRIED LIFE

Von moved in three weeks ago.

We'll be evicted from my apartment in two days.

His hands folded sheets of newspaper over plates. I unhooked my new drapes and put them in plastic covers.

Von looked up from his task. "You think they'll take them back?"

"Their choice. Slightly used drapes or nothing. I paid a hundred down. Maybe the store can sell them, and retrieve part of the other four hundred.

A persistent knock at the door attempted to make me hurry. I didn't.

"Maybe the building is on fire," Von joked as I walked slowly to the door.

"Carthage Furniture pick-up for nonpayment." A young guy in a gray work suit announced with disapproval in his tone.

I waved my hand in an all-encompassing gesture taking in my former furniture. "Go for it!"

"Took this stuff up here eight weeks ago and here we go again. I told my dad he shouldn't trust people to make monthly payments."

His two partners headed for the sectional sofa. The mouthy

guy glared at me. "Won't be anything left when my old man retires because of deadbeats."

My hand would fit nicely around Carthage Junior's neck. Unfortunately, Von intervened before I choked the guy.

"Get it and get out. Lost her job. No fault of her own. You must live in a vacuum if you don't know that the economy sucks. Maybe someday you'll get out of your daddy's pocket, and live in the real world with the rest of us."

Carthage Junior brought up an unfriendly finger that disappeared into a fist.

"Shut up fag."

Von taunted, "See yourself in me, hey?"

The older worker grabbed Carthage from behind as he lurched toward Von.

"Take a side table and wait downstairs," he ordered.

For some reason owner junior did as told.

"Sorry," the older man said. "Kids got an attitude to match his temper. We'll get this stuff out of your way."

They worked silently moving every piece into the hall. The older guy handed me a copy of the repossession sheet. I signed, then closed the door on my exiting furniture.

"We have a dance floor," Von commented.

I remembered Grandma singing "Happy Days are Here Again" and I changed it to fit our situation. I bowed, Von curtsied then we danced around the room while I sang "Happy Days Aren't Here Again."

Von's cell phone interrupted our hectic pity dance.

His eyes lifted to mine as he said, "Hello Mom."

He pushed the speaker button, and placed the phone on the breakfast bar. Each of us mounted a barstool.

"Von, your dad agreed you may come home if you don't act weird. None of that sissy stuff, or he'll put out your lights."

The woman's voice was fast and frantic. Made me wonder if she'd actually gotten her husband's approval.

A "poor me" tone seeped into her words. "I sent the money this morning through Western Union. Not enough to fly, but plenty for the bus. I've been saving money for a trip to see my sister. Maybe you'll pay me back as soon as you get a job?"

"I will Mom," he promised.

"Dad said he's not running a charity, so you'll have to contribute."

"Does he have work I can do at the garage? I know computers and clerical stuff."

"It's too embarrassing to have his workers know he has a son who isn't a real man. You'll have to look elsewhere."

Von pressed an escaped tear into his cheek. "Sure Mom, I understand. I'll phone when I get to the bus station."

"About that, I'm cleaning houses. If it's between eight and five you'll need to wait at the station until I get off work."

"Okay," Von gulped. "See you soon."

I expected him to cry or scream. He did neither.

"Going backward on my life's journey," he stated.

"That's two of us."

"Maybe I can leave early tomorrow."

"I forbid it Von. You must stay with me as long as possible. I need one more day with my best friend. One less day of putting up with other people."

"Is the woman you're staying with hard to get along with? What's her name—Julie?"

"She's okay," I lied.

"I'll help you move the rest of your stuff to her apartment," he offered.

"No, she has her own dishes and furniture. My belongings would be in her way."

"What are you going to do with your things?"

"Going to ask Fred if he has a place to store them until I get back on my feet."

"You could sell the bedroom set."

"I'll need a place to sleep when I can afford my own place. Probably couldn't get much for it anyway."

"I have to check on the bus schedule," Von said.

"You do that while I catch up on our laundry."

I took the stairs instead of the elevator. My only exercise routine since the hurricane of my life left me too depressed to pretend to give a shit about anything including my appearance.

The clothes divided among three washers I stared as the contents bathed in bubbles. A tattered magazine sat on the chair beside me, but it required too much effort to pick up much less read.

Something in the pit of my stomach tried to force me to confront my lie to Von. Julie, my nonexistent friend with an apartment, was contrived to assure Von I was okay. It also kept pity at bay from anyone inquiring as to my wellbeing.

Actually, my new home was my red Mustang. My bathroom was the all night truck stop. A container of Tide hitting the floor interrupted my musings.

Fred had come in, losing control of his clothesbasket. After retrieving the detergent, I grabbed the bleach before it toppled off the top. He could pick up his stained underwear.

"Thanks, Marcy."

"Welcome."

"I shouldn't put off the laundry so long."

"Easy to ignore," I offered.

"Heard you going down the steps. Inspired me to collect my dirty stuff." Sweat beads formed across his forehead.

"Glad I'm an inspiration."

"You're so beautiful I can hardly keep my eyes off you." Lines of wetness appeared under his arms, and spread into ovals.

"My dad said that inner beauty is what counts." My words were already wary, my brain tired of forcing conversation.

"He was looking at you as a father, not as a heterosexual male."

Creepy. "Been meaning to ask if you have storage space available on credit. I'm moving in with a friend, but I want a storage unit for extra stuff."

"Got an empty unit three miles away."

"What's the charge?"

"The chance to look at you." His stare clung to my boobs.

Irritation crept into my body. "What does that mean?"

"To see your breasts would make me the happiest man alive." A smile stretched across his yellowed teeth.

My body tightened as I stepped away from him. "Forget it, Fred. I want storage, not to be molested."

"Six months free rent for six minutes loving your breasts. That's like earning $150 a minute. Can't beat that deal."

I watched as Fred stuffed laundry into four washers. I moved my loads into dryers. He left and returned five minutes later. I grasped the storage lock and key he handed me, unit 13 in small red letters. I'd not actually agreed, but the absence of a "no" must mean "yes." There was no alternative for my penniless state of existence. I was damaged goods, and after Theo, a boob-kissing freak seemed harmless.

"Ready?" His breathy voice questioned.

I nodded.

The restroom door creaked as it opened. I entered first. I fumbled with the top button on my shirt, but his hand squeezed over mine until it dropped. He unbuttoned slowly as if savoring each second. Long, dirty-nailed, fingers easily manipulated each button. He slipped the garment from my shoulders and unfastened my bra.

I looked at the floor avoiding eye contact. A needless activity as a glimpse of his face revealed my boobs mesmerized him. He caressed each one as a welcoming gesture. Then smoothed my nipples, perhaps hoping they'd pop-up in response to his touch. Instead they retreated further into their brown caverns.

Rapid, slobbery kisses covered my right boob, then the left. Sweat dripped from his forehead onto the cold unrelenting surface of my chest.

A soggy, partially opened shirt revealed a mass of black and gray hairs standing on end. One sweaty hand massaged my left tit as he sucked the right one. He pulled it from his mouth and flicked my unyielding nipple with his finger.

"Damn it! Come out!" he ordered.

My body tensed, jerked. Chill bumps erupted on my chest.

"Cold, frigid woman," he yipped.

One hand pulled my sweat pants downward while the other hand plastered me against the wall.

"Not getting enough for my money." He spit the words into my face.

"No," I yelped.

The restroom door rattled. The lock held for a minute then the door was ripped off the hinges. Samuel stood wide legged in the opening. His hands yanked Fred from the small room, and clamped him against the wall. "I'm going to break your neck, bastard."

"Please don't hurt him. I let him," I panted.

Samuel's hand dropped from Fred's neck. His glance fell

momentarily on my bare chest. Fred scampered out like a crazed animal.

I fumbled buttons into holes, pushed the damp laundry into the basket, and ran out of the laundry under Samuel's grinding stare.

His two words followed me out the door, "Scraping bottom."

CHAPTER SIX

SCRAPING BOTTOM

The day came quickly—farewell to Von. He nodded in my direction before he tackled two suitcases through the bus station's double glass door. He dyed his auburn hair to brunette, and got a manly cut. A Cardinal's T-shirt, black jogging pants and Nikes completed his look. Now he looked like an ordinary guy, not my friend, the extraordinary gay.

I parked the Mustang in a no parking zone, and slid from the seat to run after him. "Von," I hollered across the waiting area. Multiple eyes turned toward me.

He turned a face twisted with sadness and soaked with tears.

"I love you, my friend, and someday we'll be back together—I promise."

The suitcases hit the floor and fell sideways. I imagine that the scattering of people in the bus terminal thought we were parting lovers. Perhaps some understand it's more difficult to part with a best friend than a sex partner.

I planted a ferocious hug then softly pecked his lips.

"That'll keep me going Marcy until we meet again," he promised.

"You better not cheat on me," I warned. "Don't be finding a

new BFF."

"Not to worry! You're my one and only." He assured me, then leaned in with a soft whisper in my ear, "I have on a thong beneath my hetero uniform."

A giggle burst out. "Glad to hear you've got a bit of your true self close."

Another whisper, "Didn't want to confuse my private parts."

I laughed again and kissed his cheek. "Get out of here so you can head back sooner."

Back in the Mustang I laid my head on the steering wheel, and let waves of contained emotion seethe out for thirty minutes.

Finally, I straightened my back, smoothed down my wild hairdo and told myself enough moaning and groaning. I'd soon get settled in a new job and bring Von home. Time to get my stuff out before the manager threw it on the pavement.

———◆———

Samuel climbed out of his truck when I pulled up behind him in front of the apartment building. Von asked him to help move my stuff to storage. I didn't have the guts after our encounter in the laundry room. Perhaps I should clear the air but at this point there was too much pollution between us.

Once upstairs he started dismantling the bed. I carried the nightstands to the hall and covered the lamps in bubble wrap. Also, pulled the boxes of dishes, towels, and linens into the hall. Most of my clothes already packed. Essentials were tucked away in my car trunk early this morning.

We managed to transport the first load to street level. I blocked the elevator door to have extra time to get the dresser out. Luckily a muscular male tenant happened to come in as I struggled with my end of the dresser. He took over without comment. The men easily lifted the furniture into the truck. They left me to guard as they brought down another elevator load.

"Truck's full," Samuel announced.

The two left to deposit my life into a metal container. An

hour later they returned and filled the truck again.

Muscular guy had to leave for work. After much thanks to him, I got in the truck seat for my dreaded journey with Sam.

"Thank you for trying to rescue me from Fred," I said meekly.

His eyes caught me with a side-glance. "Next time don't get into predicaments."

"I know I was a fool. Sorry, I disappointed you."

"You disappointed yourself," he growled.

My voice agitated, "Your judgment aside—sometimes a woman just has to survive."

"You're right."

I didn't expect agreement from that sour face.

He quickly changed the subject. "Did Von get off okay?"

"Yes, sad day for us."

"A good guy," he said. A shadow of regret distorted his features.

"The best."

"Von said that you're moving in with a friend, Judy?"

"Hopefully, not for long. Judy isn't the easiest person to live with."

His head turned to deliver a steel look. "Actually, Von said her name is Julie."

Caught, I sat silently.

"Became a private eye when I left the police force. I pay attention when stories don't match."

"Didn't want Von to worry about me and my choices."

"So you're moving in with some sex-crazed lunatic?"

"I'm tired of this conversation, Samuel, butt out."

"Gladly," he said.

We talked about the sunny weather and dreary economy as we completed our trip back to the apartment.

"I'm going up for one final walk through. Thanks so much for helping me."

"Good luck to you," he said.

I stopped in the exercise room. Lifting weights and running on the treadmill activated a little energy. One floor up I bought a Snickers bar from the machine. I walked slowly up the stairs counting steps as I went. My key turned the door lock for the final time.

I retrieved a bottle with a few ounces of wine from the fridge. I sat on the floor and watched the sidewalk traffic. A bird landed on the window ledge and nodded his head.

A swig of wine, a bite of candy—my official goodbye to the good life. The next resident took ownership at 3 p.m. At 2:45 I took the last swallow of wine, and smashed the bottle on the window ledge. I held the shagged bottleneck, and looked at my reflection in the picture window as I aimed the points toward my throat. The easy way out.

CHAPTER SEVEN

HOMELESS

Two weeks living in a car left my back achy, my body grimy, and my eyes baggy.

I choose a new lot every night, hoping to avoid cops checking suspicious vehicles. That night I was parked at the side of an all-night grocery. I'd already gone in to pee and brush my teeth.

I spoofed the quilt like a tent around me. A stick served as my hoisting device. This strange pyramid of patchwork fabric in the back seat hid me from passers-by.

My head settled into my pillow—I listened. Don't know if I'll ever get used to the constant prospect of sudden danger breaking through the window. My second night, I woke to a male teen peering into my mess, crowbar in hand. My voice screeched and moaned beneath my cover. As if having sex, with a strong, mean man. The intruder scampered away perhaps afraid of things that moan in the night. There was no night when sleep came easy but that night was even worse. My scalp was itchy from four days without a shower. My brain focused on the fact my access to the outside world—my cell phone—would be turned off next week. No one can even phone if they want to hire me.

Sold blood and six inches of my hair was wacked. At least they went to good causes. Learning to live in poverty is a life lesson—pay now and pray a few bucks will show up later.

Earlier that day I smiled at an old woman, who lined up behind me at McDonalds. The lines on her face mapped a long life. She didn't speak. I turned my focus to the menu. My eyes browsed the list. It seemed like a carnival of culinary delight.

My last two dollars handed toward the attendant for a small order of fries and a diet coke—my caffeine boost.

"Not enough here," the guy said.

"Okay, forget the fries." *No need to check my purse, all my change long gone.*

A little later, the gray haired lady set a big breakfast in front of me.

"You shouldn't have," I said.

"Your smile brightened an old woman's day. Don't give up, child." She waved an arthritis-crippled hand as she turned away.

The king's feast before me I ate ravished then slowed my pace. *Save half* I told myself.

That night I finished my stiff pancake, bumpy eggs, and one slice of brittle bacon. I was thankful that I'd come to my senses before devouring the day's only meal at one sitting.

My partially full belly kept sleep even more distant. The lot too quiet, lights too dim, and night too black.

The first gentle sprinkles turned to walloping splatters against my front window. My uneasiness increased with the storm.

The door handle rattled. Breath huffed from deep within my chest. I squeezed my hand against my mouth to suppress my desire to scream. I peeped from beneath my quilt tent. Black eye make-up mixed with blood curled down her face. A frightened animal she scratched at the window. Her sunken eyes begged without words.

"Go away!"

"He'll kill me."

First, I opened the door. Second, I realized I might soon die. I stuttered, "Where is he?"

"Paying for beer."

My feet clamored toward the back of the car. I popped the trunk. The stranger crawled in without a word, and moved into a fetal position in the midst of my junk.

Back behind the wheel the engine sputtered and my heart joined in.

A man appeared in front of the Mustang. The parking lot light illuminated his wildly waving arms and deranged expression.

I rolled the window down a couple of inches and hollered after a thunderbolt. "You've got two seconds to move before you're flattened on the pavement. The engine roared as I revved without releasing the brake. He ran forward and clutched my door handle. His fingers gripped the open slot at the top of the glass.

Chewing tobacco dribbled down into his chin stubble. "Not goin' to hurt you, bitch. Lookin' for my woman. Did you see which way she went?"

I blasted my words above the thunder. "Hell, as fast as she ran into those trees, you must be a monster." *Maybe loudness helps camouflage lies.*

I held my phone in his field of vision and punched a nine then a one. He scampered toward the brush before the last number was pushed.

Trembles assaulted my body. Not sure where to go.

Ten minutes of aimless driving and my brain released fear mode. The location of the police station popped into my head. Five minutes later I parked under the bright lights at the station's front entrance. An officer, who looked a couple years older than me, halted my car exit.

Can't park here," he snapped

"Must get her out," I shouted.

He walked toward me. "Out?"

"My trunk." I brushed against him as I trotted forward.

His steps scrambled the gravel as he followed me.

A bloody-faced woman met his gaze as I lifted the trunk lid.

"Whoa," the officer said. "What's this about?"

My words rushed out. "Some lunatic threatened her. I hid her in my trunk before he killed her."

A scowl distorted his mouth. "Did you have a magic

shield to protect yourself?"

"Well Officer Scarlatti," I read his faded nametag. "Should I have left her?"

"Probably, you don't look big enough to stop anything."

His patronizing tone sent my blood pressure upward. "It wasn't hand-to-hand combat."

"Be thankful for that," he shot back.

His hands supported the woman's body as she climbed from the trunk.

"Come in," Scarlatti ordered. "You need to fill out paperwork on the aggressor."

Her head moved side to side.

"That guy needs stopped," I yelped.

"No," she squeaked as her hand smeared streaks of blood and mascara down the side of her face.

The cop's voice rose above the thunder. "If you aren't going to press charges we can't arrest him."

I heard disgust in the officer's tone and I felt the same thing rising in my gut. *I risked my life, or at least pain and suffering for this female wimp.*

He tromped toward his patrol car.

I ran behind him, "What am I supposed to do with her?"

"There's a domestic violence shelter at Third and Lexington. The cruiser door slammed, the tires squealed, and Scarlatti was history.

"Get in the back seat and stay down," I directed through clenched teeth.

She whimpered, "You taking me to your place?"

"This car is my home."

"You shittin' me? Don't look like the type."

"Not sure what type that is, but I'm jobless, homeless and moneyless. I guess new poverty is what the newspaper calls it."

I'm sure passers-by thought I was a crazy woman as I continued chatting with my hidden company.

"What's your name?"

"Sidney Mackie."

"I'm Marcy." I handed back a wad of McDonald's napkins.

She blotted the blood on her face. "Appreciate you protecting me."

"I can't help anymore. Cop told me where to drop you off."

"I've been at the Women's Shelter a few times."

My argumentative words blurted. "So your husband beats you regularly?"

Sidney ignored the sarcasm.

"Every chance he gets. If dinner isn't on the table at 6 p.m. When we run out of beer, which is what happened tonight. If his work pants don't have a crease down the front. Not married to him, but he considers me his woman."

"I'd consider him long gone."

"I got nothin' else, Marcy."

"You love this guy, Sidney?"

"Never loved anyone. I got food and a roof over my head," she said warily.

"Not worth it," I chimed.

"Better than you got." Her words bit.

I glanced at her from my rear view mirror. "Well, I got nothing and you have a woman beater. I'll stick with nothing."

She gulped. "You don't know about my life."

"True," I said calmly. An effort to stop her tears.

"Here we are," I announced.

"Come in with me?" Her bottom lip quivered. "They might not take me."

Sidney and I made our way to the front door.

After a couple of knocks a light glared above our heads. A pair of eyes peered from the small glass peek window.

A lock rolled, a chain rattled, and the door cautiously opened.

"Sidney," the woman said. She appeared to be in her fifties—short black hair, olive skin, tall and slender. Based on the kindness in her face and tone, someone accustomed to beaten women appearing in the night.

Sidney didn't respond. So I did, "Officer said to bring her here. She wouldn't press charges against the monster. He beat her."

"Sid, you know where the clean clothes are stored. Take a shower so we can see what first aid you need."

Sid walked toward a narrow hall. No thanks crossed her lips.

"I don't get it," I grumbled. "Why doesn't she leave him?"

"Your name?"

"Marcy Simon."

"Domestic violence statistics show the guy is more likely to murder her if she deserts him. It's easy to tell her to run away, but the truth is she may be signing her own death certificate."

"Sorry—didn't realize. I better head out."

"Home?"

"Don't have one." I'd spouted my secret without thinking.

Her facial expression didn't change, as if she already knew my lot in life.

"Then you must stay tonight. The lightning and thunder are already here and flooding is expected."

I stood silent.

"I'll wait by the front door while you get your things."

My teeth chattered as lightning illuminated my path. Opening my trunk I stuffed necessities into a paper bag and returned to my hostess.

I trailed her down the same hall where Sid disappeared.

"Showers on the left and upstairs," she pointed. "On the right is a mini laundry. Kitchen is at the end of the hall. Up the stairwell to the right is your room, number 22."

I squeezed the brown bag against my chest and ascended the stairs. The open door revealed a small room. A tattered, flowered comforter covered the twin bed. I bent and smelled its surface—clean.

Lightning flashed outside the window. I pulled the frayed edges of the turquoise drapes together. The room wasn't much bigger than my former walk-in closet. A bed, a nightstand, and a cracked lamp filled the room.

A gentle knock on the door.

"Marcy."

"Yes," I cracked the door open.

"Forgot to introduce myself. I'm Sonya. Here's a clean gown for you."

Is Sonya a psychic? She seemed to know my circumstance before I told her. Perhaps I should escape while I have a chance. Too tired. Too stormy.

The gown tossed over my shoulder I walked to the shower.

Shower water sprayed its comforting warmness. I scrubbed the shampoo into my sheared hair. Felt like a poor woman's spa treatment.

The rough towel soaked up my wetness before I stuck my head through the opening on the flowered gown. The flowers once red now turned pink.

I heard a baby crying down the hall as I reentered my sleeping space.

The pillow fluffed, the covers turned back I snuggled into the warm softness of the mattress. Rain pitter-pattered against the roof then turned to bold strikes. My eyes closed.

———◆———

I awoke to a persistent knock and a lilting voice. "Time to get up."

I'd slept until 10 a.m. A bed is certainly a good sleep aid. I pulled the least dingy underwear and clothes from my bag.

I made my way down the steps. Downstairs noises blended from a couple of rooms. I turned into the kitchen.

Twinkling eyes and a mouth brightened by red lipstick greeted me. "Get yourself a bowl of cereal. You missed breakfast." Her finger pointed to a cabinet.

I ate as she scrubbed plates. A couple of gray curls escaped from her bun and hung loosely at her shoulders. She was probably in her mid sixties and huggably soft.

My breakfast quickly finished I spied a red checked dishcloth and dried dishes that dripped on a towel beside the sink.

"What are you doing here, child?"

"Dropped off Sid and spent the night."

"Why didn't you go home?"

"I don't have one. Run of bad luck. Laid off at work. Are there any job openings?"

"Nope, all volunteers. There's an opening for a waitress at Dinah's Rockin' Diner three miles east of here."

"No experience," I said and reached for a big iron pot.

"They train. Free meal every day. Low pay, but some folks tip good."

"I'll give it a try."

"Tell them Maybelle sent you."

My hostess from the night before entered the kitchen.

"Marcy, I'm Sonya Yates. Can't remember if I introduced myself last night."

"You did. I'll leave within the hour."

"No hurry. You may stay a month," Sonya offered.

"I don't want to take someone's place."

"You won't be," Maybelle inserted. "With the cold weather coming, you might as well light here for a spell."

"You're sure you can spare the room?"

Sonya's eyes met mine, "Positive."

"Maybelle told me about a waitress opening. I'll check it out as soon as I have clean clothes."

"Oh my gosh, I forgot." Sonya's finger thumped her forehead. "Sidney is on the phone for you."

I followed Sonya to her office. Her turquoise drapes were twins to the ones in my room. A brick held up one desk leg. The shag carpet an array of earthen shades darkened by years of wear. I seated myself in a cracked leather chair.

"Hello," I said into the rotary phone.

"It's Sidney. I'm going to do it—leave him. Packing my stuff and taking off. Brother coming to help me."

"Good for you," I said.

The conversation ended, pride puffed my chest. I'd obviously given her a bravery boost yesterday, a powerful feeling for her and me both.

I retrieved my dirty clothes from upstairs and my car. All four washers were filled, but no one waited. I let my guilt pass in order to get my laundry done, because a clean outfit was a job interview necessity.

———— ✦ ————

A white blouse and black slacks were my interview clothes. Wasn't hard to find the restaurant, but the trucks that lined the street in front of Dinah's left me nowhere to park but three blocks away.

The place was decorated like a fifties diner. A flashing sign out front advertised, "Fifties Fare." Only two bar stools were unoccupied. A jukebox played "Love Me Tender."

A man in a corner booth complained. "You're making me late for work."

A doughy-faced, familiar-looking woman responded. "Don't get your underwear in a knot, Ivan. We're doin' the best we can. New hire didn't show this morning."

I lined up behind four others in the cash register line. Finally, my turn, "I'd like to apply for the waitress job."

She eyed me, "You got any experience?"

"None, but I'm a fast learner."

"No time for babysitting, I need someone who can hit the ground running.'"

"Please give me a chance. Maybelle sent me."

Her cheeks puffed. "I need to keep this business going, in spite of my sister sending over anyone who looks hungry." She waved me aside to ring up the next ticket.

I put my butt on the only empty stool. *That's why she looked familiar—Maybelle's sister.*

Looked like identical twins, except one had straight hair and the other curly. One wore a sneer and the other a smile.

I surveyed the restaurant—worn—but fun. Polka dot pink seat covers, and wooden tables covered by white butcher paper for scribbling. An old-fashioned black and white tiled floor. Posters decorated every wall—Elvis and Fats Domino the obvious favorites. No one offered me a menu.

Voices raised an octave or two as customers called for coffee, water, whatever.

The jukebox started playing "Rockin' Robin" and it apparently gave me courage. I jumped off the stool. Spied the table cleaning gurney and preceded to stack dishes and glasses, then wipe the tables clean.

When I passed a voice requested a coffee refill. I speed walked across the room and managed to restrain from rocking out with the beat.

"For you sir."

He gave a garbled thank you.

A woman ordered water, another wanted juice, a different kind of syrup and still another wanted to gripe. A two-year-old spilled her milk, which saved me from the complainer.

Scurrying from one job to the next, I didn't check on the boss's temperature. Cold, hot, or warm didn't matter. I'd already been dismissed. Not likely she'd phone the cops because a stranger scrubbed her tables.

At one-thirty the business slowed. I poured my own glass of water. Oops, the boss stared from over the top of the cash register.

The fleshy face formed into a smile. "You're a little whippersnapper. Got some balls working like you got a job here."

"That song, 'Rockin' Robin,' made me lose control."

"I'll give you a shake. Saved us today. Pay is minimum wage plus tips. Don't be hateful to the customers even if it's their fault. Treat them like gold cause they are in this economy."

Dinah, my new boss, ran through procedures at a clipped pace. I followed her into the kitchen to meet the cook.

"We call him Elvis," Dinah explained, "because he's obsessed with the guy."

His real name is Washington Carver Washington."

"My dad had quite a sense of humor," Elvis explained in a southern drawl.

Elvis probably wouldn't fit anywhere but a fifty's diner or Las Vegas. Long sideburns, tight pants, and a jeweled collar poked out from the neck of his white chef's jacket.

"Waitress is Ginny," Dinah said. "She left to take her son from kindergarten to daycare, back in a few. Busboy is Clive. Out sick today. Don't think as fast as some folks, but he's a hard worker. Well, that's the gang. Except for my sister, Maybelle, who works night shift."

"She told me about the restaurant. Met her this morning at the shelter."

"You hiding from an abuser?"

"No, staying there a few days while I get back on my feet."

"Any sign of drugs or alcohol and you're history." Dinah's voice cut the air between us.

"No problem here."

"You're officially the new girl."

I wrapped my arms around her soft girth and gave her a hug. She stiffened, but then laughed as I pulled away. "Sorry," I muttered.

"Next week you'll want to strangle me. I'll take a hug while I can."

CHAPTER EIGHT

BLOOM WHERE PLANTED

I forced myself out of the twin bed and into the upstairs shower. Ten hours at Dinah's restaurant the day before left me feeling like a wilted plant. Never worked so hard.

Six in the morning and all was quiet. I dressed in rolled-up blue jeans and a pink polka dot top supplied by Dinah. My hair was too short for a ponytail, so I slicked it back before brushing my bangs into an Elvis sideswipe. Old running shoes substituted for sneakers.

Ten minutes ahead of schedule, I cautiously inspected the view from the front door peek window—as instructed. No deranged abusers loitered out front. I fetched the newspaper, and then sunk onto the top step as I recognized the dark eyes that stared from the front cover. The paper trembled in my hands.

HOMICIDE SUSPECTED IN WOMAN'S DEATH, the headline announced. "Sidney Mackie, age twenty-seven, was found dead at her place of residence yesterday evening. Neighbors reported that her brother, Jerry Mackie, was seen at the home earlier in the day. An unidentified source said the siblings argued in the front yard. Mackie's common law husband, Don Bethel, reported he found Sidney's body in the bathtub when he arrived home from work. Bethel said the victim's brother was the likely killer. He referred to Jerry Mackie as a drunken bum who threatened to hurt Sidney, when she refused to loan him money."

I caused this—made her feel weak because she didn't run from the monster. A groan escaped my throat. Bethel probably set up the guy but maybe the brother did kill her. There was a witness that they argued. Maybe both men are wackos. No way for me to know.

I glanced at my watch and trotted to my purse. I dropped the newspaper on the side table. Even this was no excuse for lateness on my second day at work. My emotional stupor needed to be hidden before I arrived at the restaurant

———— ◆ ————

"Check the salt and pepper dispensers." Dinah directed as I came in the door.

"Look a little gloomy, girl." Sounded more like a warning than concern.

"I knew that woman who was murdered, Sidney Mackie. Sucks her life was so short."

"For sure," Dinah agreed, "but past the time to worry about her. Let's feed the living."

Fake Elvis slipped coins into the machine and started real Elvis. "Hound Dog" propelled me to chores and away from guilt.

The morning was fast and furious. I was amazed at the number of men who frequented the pink girlie establishment. When the food was good, it apparently didn't threaten your manhood to sit on polka dot chairs. Chunks of conversations revealed football games, fighters, and big machines as the main topics. A couple of them tugged at their crouches maybe making sure a penis hadn't evaporated in the girlie environment.

"You're new here," a young woman stated. Her bangs were backcombed three inches—a rainbow of shades: red, black and blond. Her eyebrows were thin lines of red that matched a few bang strands. Hot pants sunk into her butt crack and her boobs threatened to pop out.

"Yes, started yesterday. You okay sitting at the bar?"

She followed to an empty stool. A couple of wolf whistles sounded from the corner table. Her fingers flittered in that direction, "Hi guys."

Seated, I handed her a menu.

She waved it off. "Just a slice of toast and a Pepsi. Short on funds. No johns last night. Business is slow."

"Ah," I said.

"Don't judge me. Your work is like slave labor. I have fun," she shrilled.

"Surprised by your honesty, no judgment intended. I'm Marcy. What's your name?"

"I go by Barbee. My real name is Barbara. I needed a fun name in my line of work. Some women at the apartment complex call me Little Whore."

My brain locked, too much information. "I'll get your order in. Dinah's giving me the look."

"You go, girl," Barbee directed. As if I was the child when she probably hadn't reach twenty years.

When I returned, she was too busy massaging the right arm of a city utility guy to continue our conversation.

By two o'clock business slowed. The door creaked open. A man folded his huge frame into the far corner booth. Half his face was a puckered red blotch that rounded a fake eye.

His good eye caught my gaze. It stared for a second, and then focused on the jukebox. Pity, dread, discomfort bubbled inside me.

I gave a menu to the man.

"You look a little queasy." He read my nametag, "Marcy."

My eyes peered above his head. "Been a busy morning."

"I'm thinking you've never seen a man as handsome as me."

I looked into his good eye. "Thank goodness you finally showed. Now I've got someone to compare the others to."

He laughed, "Pretty quick on your feet, Marcy."

The low masculine tone said my name with familiarity.

"Are you eating today, sir?"

"Burger and fries, no cheese."

"Drink?"

"Coffee. By the way, I'm Earl."

"Glad to meet you. A regular?"

"Yes, after a while you may even look at my face without wincing."

"Already there."

Not sure why, but I smiled as I handed the order to Elvis.

———— ◆ ————

Six hours later, I knocked on Sonya's office door. "You got a minute?"

I slouched in a chair across from her.

The newspaper was opened on her desk. The ache in my chest returned.

"I... I feel like I provoked Sidney to leave her guy. Questioned why she'd stay with the jerk. Now she's dead."

"We make our own decisions, Marcy. You happened to show-up right before she'd had all she could take. Don't think your influence was more than a smidgen of why she bolted. Anyway, the paper indicated her brother did it, not Bethel."

"She told me her brother offered to help her. Now I'm afraid Bethel is setting him up."

"Something you should tell Officer Scarlatti."

"You know him?"

"Zane's my son. My last name is different because I remarried after I divorced his dad. Zane's the one who told me that you lived in your car."

"I thought you had magical powers."

A smile played at her lips. "I wish. I'd turn the world around for the women who come through the front door."

"An interesting goal," I responded.

"Zane saw you parked on various parking lots overnight."

"He speculated I was a damsel in distress?" I felt my anger rise at the prospect of a man considering me weak and helpless.

Sonya tapped her pen on the desk. "Lot of broken women around these parts. He and his fellow officers are frequently the eyes and ears for this facility."

"Sorry for the attitude. I have big time man issues."

"Common around here. Have you developed a future plan?"

"I'll apply for student loans."

"Finish your education. Good idea."

I rose and moved toward the door, then turned back. "Who knows, I may help women turn their lives around!"

SIX YEARS LATER

CHAPTER NINE

A NEW LIFE

Even though I'm a psychologist, I hadn't figured out why I was obsessed to rent my old apartment. After six months in the city, I moved back to my friends and town. Another four months before my old apartment was vacated. Only forty minutes from my city office, and wealthy clients, the move didn't impact my practice. The Women's Shelter is where I spend most Saturdays.

That day I had an appointment scheduled with my psychiatrist. A woman assigned, by my college advisor, to put me through mandatory therapy during my last year of graduate school. They wanted psychologists to "heal thyself" before working with other people—a good plan.

Didn't like my therapist, Celeste Thomas, but she already spent a semester listening to my history, which should result in faster conclusions.

I pulled on tan slacks and a blue blouse. My hair lay loose on my shoulders. At work I wear it up, which I think helps me look older, more professional.

Thoughts swirled in my head as I drove my newly painted Mustang toward her office. Celeste didn't usually see clients on Fridays but made an exception for me, although she warned I'd owe her a favor. She worked under rules of confidentiality. I could tell my secrets without her blabbing them all over town.

It was a familiar walk from my car, up the elevator, and down the hall to her office. I knocked on the door, "Hello."

"Come in," she responded.

Celeste wore tight jeans, brown-laced fashion boots, and a green shirt that set her green eyes sparkling. Her short black hair was spiked in the front.

"What's up, Marcy?"

"Thanks for seeing me today."

"You'll have an opportunity to pay me back."

I stiffened. Owing Celeste a favor for this free weekend session seemed a bit ominous. Oh well, too late now.

"I'm considering a side endeavor," I divulged.

"Besides therapy?"

"Related. Sounds ridiculous when I say it out loud. But I want to help women get rid of jerks in their lives—cheaters, bullies, abusers."

"You want advice on murdering bad guys?" Sarcasm mingled with her forced laugh.

"Of course not. Strange as it sounds, I came to ask if I'm crazy."

Her tone flattened. "You still have unresolved man issues. Perhaps I shouldn't have signed that mental health statement that your graduate school required."

Speechless, I looked at the crystal penholder on her desk. *Maybe I shouldn't have confided in this woman.*

'I'm screwing with you, Marcy. More power to you if you can disengage women from chronic jerks."

"I guess..."

Her stare dug into my soul. "Why are you really here?"

"The bottom line—how sick is revenge? I consider myself a mentally healthy person but occasionally hate swells up inside. I think I could actually kill the man who raped me. At least once a month I think about ways to murder him without getting caught. Fantasies of a hole in his head, and blood rushing out his ears interrupt my life. It's like an angry tyrant inside my brain working to get out."

"Don't you think it's time to stop the past from molding your future?"

Flippant words popped from my mouth. "Too late. Already has."

"You need to move on, Marcy."

"I can't. The memory never fades."

"He never paid," Celeste summarized, "so these other bad men will?"

"They'll pay for their own sins. No one can pay Theo's debt."

Celeste switched to a stern professional face. "Back to your revenge question. At a high level it's a learning tool to teach an aggressor there are repercussions for their behavior. But at a lower level there's no correction or learning for the perpetrator. So the revenge becomes a person acting on personal hate—yours in this case."

I didn't respond.

"Which means, Marcy, you need to decide the road you'll take. Take the low road and you get revenge. On the high road you help women without punishing their partners. Sounds like you need to make a choice. We both know this 'man hatred' originated from the molestation by your former boss."

I stood, and glanced past her through the window behind her desk. "Something to think about. Thank you, again."

Celeste followed me to the door. "Let's do lunch."

"Psychologists aren't allowed to interact socially with clients."

Celeste ignored the ethics issue. "We're colleagues. Week from Monday work for you?"

"Sure." I agreed to the last thing I wanted.

Tepid air in the parking lot warmed my body but not my heart. My mind considered the alternatives Celeste proposed. I didn't really understand why I came. Validation, I guess. Someone to assure me it was okay to take the low road, when dealing with abusive men.

I drove home without realizing I did so. How I missed Von in times like these. My best friend would understand why Theo and all his cruel male counterparts deserved to suffer for their abuse of women.

Von and I talked a few times after he moved home. After a couple of months, his mother said he'd moved out and didn't leave a forwarding number. I filled my time with waitressing and getting an education positive he'd eventually call me.

It was time to fulfill my promise to bring Von home—but first I had to find him.

————◆————

Back in my apartment, I dug my old address book out of the junk drawer. There it was, the home address of his parents, Ben and Ursula Sandburg. My finger poked the numbers into the phone. A shrill female voice answered.

"Is this Ursula Sandburg?"

"Who wants to know?"

"Marcy Simon. I'm tracking down your son, Von."

No response. I waited.

Sarcasm blended into her tone. "Knew someone by that name, but he's long gone."

My chest tightened. "He died?"

"My husband says he's dead."

"What about you, Ursula?"

"Ain't fighting with Ben over the queer boy. Von didn't belong with normal folks."

"Where is he?"

"Don't know."

I forced myself to control the venom rising in my body. "What's your guess?"

"Few months ago a cop spotted Von under a bridge downtown. The policeman thought we might want to rescue him."

My voice cracked, "Homeless?"

"Ben said the boy got his just desserts for sinning against the rightful order of God's creation."

My anger leached out. "You two are in danger of hell fire for deserting your son."

"Well, I never," Ursula huffed.

"What would Jesus do?" I shouted, then pushed the off button.

Juvenile perhaps but I felt better.

CHAPTER TEN

TESSA, BRUISED AND BROKEN

The door creaked, and Sonya leaned into the shelter's kitchen. "Woman sitting out front. She one of yours?"

"Probably." I finished my last coffee gulp, and waved off Maybelle's offer of another cup.

Sonya stepped into the room. "Marcy, don't make any long-range client plans. Funding for the shelter was frozen until the first of the year. Without a miracle we'll close our doors in a few weeks."

"Where will the women go? Back to their abusers?" I seethed.

"Some will, others will end up on the street or with family. We're ten thousand short. Maybe we'll reopen in January."

I slowly shook my head and exited to my client.

"Tessa?" I asked as I entered the shelter's living room.

She rose slowly then reached for the hand of the little girl beside her. Marks the size of cigarette butts scarred the tops of Tessa's hands. Yellow smudged with purple under her left eye, an obvious remnant of a recent black eye.

The child, who looked to be four and turned out to be seven was a mini Tessa. Faces and arms showed no fat between flesh and bone on either. Both exhibited angular bodies with protruding elbows, and sunken cheeks under haunted eyes.

"Tessa, I'm Marcy Simon." I turned to the child. "What's your name?" Her head lowered and eyes shut.

Tessa patted the child's head. "Lilly's shy."

"Come in my office." Mother and daughter followed me through the door and sat in worn chairs facing me.

I pulled crayons and a coloring book out of a desk drawer and handed them to Tessa. "Maybe she'd like to color."

Lilly picked a pink crayon from the box. While we talked she meticulously colored roses on the princess dress.

"Tessa, what do you want to discuss?"

Her arms grasped her body, as if hugging herself. "He'll kill me someday."

"Does he hurt Lilly, too?"

"Not physically—emotionally—she sees how Jon beats me."

"Have you ever left him?"

"I've tried to escape but he always finds me. Then the beatings are twice as bad, and sometimes he chains me for a day or two. To teach me a lesson he says." She lifted her foot to show the half-inch scar that circled her ankle.

My gut twisted. "Police involved?" I queried.

"Once, but I didn't press charges." Her hands pushed against her belly. "Maddest Jon ever got—kept me chained for four days without food."

"Do you have family out of state?"

"He knows where they live. Would put them at risk if I showed up."

"How can I help you, Tessa?"

Uncertainty squeezed from narrowed lips, "I don't know."

"You're risking getting beat, or worse. You must have a reason. What life do you want for Lilly and yourself?"

Tessa's voice strained, "A life where nobody hurts us. I'm afraid all the time. Someday he'll kill me, then he'll start on Lilly. He doesn't let her have friends already. Made me home school her. What will happen to her without me?"

Foreboding rippled in my head. "Where's he today?"

"Work, but if he happens to phone home and I don't answer, he'll beat me. Doesn't let me have a cell phone."

My eyes focused on the quavering woman. "Tessa tell me

why you're here."

Resolve penetrated her fear. "For help to escape from him."

I stood abruptly. "Go home, before he figures out you're not there. I need a little time to develop a plan. Don't panic if you see a tall man with a scarred face loitering on your street. He works for me. I have your phone number and address. I'll contact you when everything is in place. Stash away anything that's important to you, like photos and jewelry."

"Clothes?"

"A last-minute grab," I advised.

"He'll murder me if he finds out." Tessa's fearful words loomed in the air.

"We'll make sure he doesn't."

Lilly's coloring halted. Her lips parted, but she didn't speak.

"Lilly," I said softly. "You need to keep our secret."

She nodded agreement. Her frightened eyes caught her mother's face. I expected tears, but instead she touched Tessa's cheek.

The pair gone, I phoned half dozen shelters. Finally found a place in North Carolina—that was far enough.

Next I phoned Earl. "Hey you, it's Marcy. You ready to work?"

"Sure thing."

I told him the abbreviated Tessa story.

Earl's words assaulted my ear. "Son-of-a-bitch, she has to give up her home, and he's the monster?"

"That's her only hope for survival. If he finds out she wasn't at home today, he'll hurt her tonight. I want your eyes and ears close."

"Trust me, they will be."

"We'll help them pack after he leaves for work Monday morning. You'll drive them to Raleigh if it works for you."

"Yes. I'll stay in touch. Purchased an old van we can use. Has a plumbing company emblem on the side."

"Sounds perfect."

"Later," he said.

I pressed my hand against my chest hoping to slow my heartbeat.

———◆———

The call came in around 8 p.m. I'd just sunk my rear into the softest chair I owned. A movie started, a glass of wine in my right hand, and a bag of popcorn in my left.

Earl's voice jolted the calm induced by the wine. "Got to move her tonight. Guy's gone crazy. I watched through the basement window. She's chained. I saw him slug her then press a cigarette butt into her arm—the bastard. I'll going after him right now."

"I'm on my way."

"Not necessary. I can handle this alone. Got to go."

Ignoring Earl's comments, I put on jeans and a T-shirt, and ran out the door.

In the car, my thoughts argued that it was unethical for a psychologist to get involved in a client's turmoil. My life mission remembered. My quest begins to help women remove male trash from their lives.

After twenty minutes, I arrived at Tessa's house. I parked a block away. I crept toward a weak square of light that shone from the basement window. I bent low, cell in hand. Ready to phone the police.

No Tessa or Lilly in sight. Earl, at six and a half feet, hung over a smaller man chained against the wall. I leaned my head against the window frame. My ear nearly touched the pane as I listened.

Jon screeched, "No man, no, you're hurting me."

Earl bellowed, "Like you hurt your little wife."

"I'm sorry, I'm sorry."

"No you're not. I saw you brutalizing her. You're a demon."

Jon's voice took on a little grit. "She took off today. Up to something. Neighbor saw her sneaking out. Tessa's my woman. I taught her a lesson."

"And I'm teaching you one." Earl lit and puffed a cigar. He fingered it then pressed the burning end into Jon's arm. "Only cowards beat women."

"Stop," Jon begged, "you're hurting me."

"Good," Earl pulled the lax chain tight, and pressed it against Jon's throat. "We're making a deal. Don't go looking for Tessa, and I won't kill you. If you ever hurt her again I'm going to saw your head off and post it out front. She's finding a new home. But me, I'm staying in town to keep an eye on you."

Earl's fist rammed into Jon's belly. "Do we have a deal?"

Jon's head shuttered the affirmative.

Earl turned toward the steps.

"Unlock me," Jon hollered.

"Your spy may come looking for you in a week or two. Hell, you may still be alive."

Heathen of me perhaps, but seeing big Earl beat the smaller man seemed the logical consequence for the bully. I found my way to the back door, and called Tessa's name as I entered.

"Here," she answered.

I found them hurriedly stuffing belongings into pillowcases.

I didn't make eye contact when Earl appeared in the doorway.

"Jon's tied up for awhile, so take anything you need."

His words would've been humorous had I not seen the brutality.

Earl picked up the television, and carried it to the fake plumbing truck.

The furniture, stained and torn, was left behind. I helped Tessa lug a mattress off the bed, and to the truck. Earl heaved it in with one firm push. We wrapped a few dishes in newspaper, threw in a couple of pots, and pushed clothes stuffed pillowcases into empty spaces in the rear of the van. The only space not filled, a single seat for Lilly.

Darkness didn't cover an occasional neighbor peeking out a window, or the old woman smoking a cigarette on the front porch across the street. She hollered, "God bless you," as Tessa got in the passenger seat.

I stood by the driver's window. "Here's four hundred for motel rooms, gas and food. Call when you get back in town."

Earl grasped the money. "Will do."

I rounded the vehicle, threw Lilly a kiss and squeezed Tessa's hand. Her head lowered and her lips grazed my hand. "You've saved our lives. I can never thank you enough."

"You have a wonderful new life. I wish you the best."

I stood and watched them disappear into the night.

The light blinked from the basement window. Tessa needed a head start, and Jon would benefit from alone time. I was happy to oblige.

"A good day!" The old lady hollered from her porch swing.

I called back, "The best."

CHAPTER ELEVEN

ENRAGED HAYLEY

I think of my city office as cozy. My office showed touches of softness and comfort. Couple of overstuffed indigo chairs and a tan sofa with two foot rests. A wall of Van Gogh fakes balanced out evenly in their space. Wood-fronted file cabinets, instead of the tasteless metal ones, lined the back wall. A bouquet of real flowers decorated the long conference table at the end of the room.

The psychologist across the hall, Damon, told me my office is too comfortable. Heavy wood furniture, and a leather sofa make his office interior stark. A glass tiger creeps across his coffee table. All things, according to Damon, that represented the hard reality of life. My clients get enough stern reality without me exhibiting it in my décor.

Not that I expected an upbeat client to come in my door—I didn't. But on that particular Monday morning, after my heart-pounding experience with Tessa, I wished for one who was at least civil. Someone unlike Hayley—she was the stiff, argumentative form who sat on the edge of the chair across from me. She appeared ready to pounce or run. Her brunette hair, pulled severely back into a ponytail, black jeans and shirt, and an upturned chin—all conveyed hostility.

Hayley's cat eyes followed my hand as I reached for a pen and writing pad. Her stare drilled into my face. I was at a loss as to how to crack the wall she placed between us.

An unprofessional stammer slipped out. "What are you doing here? I mean, how do you hope to benefit from therapy?"

Hayley leaned forward. Her eyes locked on my face. "Counseling won't help me. Didn't as a teen and never will. My husband agreed that I could skip his family reunion if I'd attend one therapy session. Told me I needed to straighten up, his words not mine."

"How does he define, 'straighten up'?"

Her words barked out. "Want a baby, come to bed, and be a happy hostess to his family and friends."

"What do you want, Hayley?" My words softened in an attempt to find a calm place in our discussion.

Her fists slammed the desk surface. "Left the hell alone. I'm who I am. He can take me or leave me. I can't be molded into his perfect woman. It's not a sin to remain childless or to watch television all night. He thinks I'm so screwed up that he manipulated me into going to a psychologist. That's why I'm here—to be fixed. But I'm not coming again. So this is it lady—one hour to cure my husband's crazy wife."

Geez. A whole hour!

"Why no children?"

"With my luck I'd end up with a female," Hayley grumbled.

"What's wrong with girls?"

"I'm a female and it sucks. I wouldn't wish that on anyone."

"Were you a sad little girl?"

"Damn, you and your questions. I don't have time to recite my life story."

"Here's an easier one. Why don't you go to bed at night?"

"Not tired."

"Are you avoiding intercourse?"

"None of your business. I meet you ten minutes ago, and you're already talking sex."

I countered, "I only have an hour, remember? What's the deal with your husband's family?"

"They want to chit-chat. Talk about clothes, and their kids birthday parties."

"What do you like to talk about?"

A guttural tone ground into her words. "Nothing, I want them to shut up. Same for you."

My left hand pulled at my ear. "Takes grit to tell a psychologist to shut up in her own office."

"That's what I'll tell my husband. It's not insanity. It's grit."

"Does he hurt you?"

"That's where you people always go. Sorry, NO."

"I think he tries to control you."

Hayley's words sprayed out with saliva. "He's not an abuser or a bastard."

"Then describe him."

Her features softened. "Heartbroken because he ended up with me instead of a sweet loving wife."

"You think you're the problem. Help me understand why you're not willing to change."

"I'm almost thirty years old and it's my life. Don't want kids. Don't want to cuddle at night. Don't want to kiss his relatives' butts. Don't want to answer any more of your stupid questions."

"I'll make a deal with you. You answer one more question, honestly, and we're finished. You'll get out of here forty minutes early. Can't beat that."

"I'd promise anything to stop this torture," Hayley sneered.

I stood and shook her limp hand, then maneuvered my body into the chair beside her. "We got a deal."

Hayley forced a yawn for affect. "Let's get this done. I'm bored."

"What's the scenario in your head when you can't sleep at night—the tape that plays over and over in your mind?"

I waited. A car's engine burped outside the window. Distant traffic hummed. Clock ticked. The room formed a cage of silence around us. Her face disappeared into her hands. When she finally lowered them, she looked toward my desk and spoke to the empty chair. Her words were soft. If I hadn't moved beside her I wouldn't have heard her story.

"He'd married my mom the day before. They didn't go on a trip because Mom, a nurse, had a hospital shift starting at six the next morning. The guy seemed like a creep from the beginning, and at fifteen I called a creep—a creep."

The faraway look in Hayley's eyes revealed she'd returned to that day.

———————◆———————

"How's my sweet new daughter?" Darren said as he crawled into my bed. "Hayley, your mom's gone to work. I want to know my girl better. Daddies need to teach their girls how to be women."

"You're a crazy bastard." My bed against the wall, I sprang forward to crawl out the end. He gripped my upper arm, and pulled me back. His left arm formed a noose around my neck.

"You got to learn your lessons little girl."

"NO."

His right hand moved like a spider over my body, touching every part. If I moved the noose tightened. After what seemed like forever he stood.

"You ever seen one of these girl"? He fondled his penis. "Trust me, you'll never get another one this good."

His body fell flat on mine. He crammed his thing into me again and again. I couldn't move from his weight. My head shook from side to side trying to keep his mouth from mine. Kissing the monster seemed even worse than the intercourse.

A rattle sounded from the front door. He bolted to his feet. His features twisted.

"Darren," my mom's lilting voice called. "Boss gave me the day off as our wedding gift."

Mom found her new husband standing in twisted jockeys next to a bed where her naked teenage daughter lay.

"Honey," Darren said, "Hayley screamed for me. I thought she was sick or someone broke in. But there she lay, naked. Begging me to screw her. I told her no way."

I pulled the sheet tightly around my body.

"She begged me to touch her. Since I'm her new daddy, she thought I'd want to know her better."

Mom sunk to the bed's edge, rage shot from her eyes.

I clutched the sheet. "He raped me, Mom."

Darren's fist punched the air. "Don't lie, Hayley. She's not going to believe that shit. Your mom knows how much I love her."

Anger turned Mom's face to ugliness. "You never liked Darren. Jealous because I found someone to love, and didn't cater to your every whim. Now you're breaking my heart."

"Mom, he hurt me."

"Pack up and get out," she screamed.

"Mama?"

"I'm not your mother anymore. I'll phone your aunt to pick you up. I'll never see your lying face again."

Darren took Mom's hand and walked from my room. As I packed I heard him banging her in the next bedroom. They didn't come out when my aunt arrived.

"I didn't lie," I told Aunt Jade.

"Never thought for a second you did," she replied. "Did he get any sperm inside you?"

"Yes," I whimpered.

"They got something called a morning after pill to stop pregnancy. I'll phone my doctor to get a prescription. How are you doing?"

"Okay," I lied.

———•———

Hayley returned to the present. Her eyes met mine. "I lived with Aunt Jade for the next three years. We never spoke of the rape."

"What happened to…"

"You promised no more questions," she said sternly.

"Sorry. No questions but please listen. I believe you have post-traumatic stress disorder."

"I thought only soldiers had that."

"Other people, who have terrifying experiences in their lives, also have PTSD."

Her eyes widened. "Does something help?"

"There's a therapy called Eye Movement Desensitization and Reprocessing—EMDR. Some psychologists have seen good results."

"Don't want drugs. So many prescribed when I was a teen I could've gotten a role as a movie zombie."

"Frequently drugs cover up problems, that they can't repair. EMDR is based on the conclusion that part of the brain constantly replays the traumatic event. The replays are warnings that you should never let the terrible thing happen again. Simply stated the trauma gets locked up in the nervous system. The therapy focuses on transferring the constant replaying of the event to a different part of the brain."

"Will it help me?"

"No guarantee, but it's worth a try." I rounded my desk, and scribbled a date and time on an appointment slip. "Same time next week."

Hayley stood and reached for the slip. Her tear-filled eyes searched my face. My arms wrapped around her, and drew her body close. She cried against my shoulder.

A few minutes later I walked her out, then flopped down into what should've been my secretary's chair. The answering machine light flickered—eight messages during Hayley's session.

The combination of no office help, plus Tessa and Hayley's traumatic situations left my body feeling like an air leaking balloon. I needed my best friend and a secretary. Von was the answer to both my prayers. The time to find him was here. I cancelled my appointments for the rest of the week, ate an apple for lunch and read the intake on my afternoon client, Eva.

CHAPTER TWELVE

LEFT BEHIND—EVA

"I've come to accept it," Eva said.

"You've reconciled that your husband left you for a woman thirty years younger?" No doubt my tone expressed disbelief.

"I think so. It hurt me. I didn't like it, but it is what it is. It's done. Frankly I'm glad Ethan's gone. Of course it took three years to develop this attitude."

I studied her face. "You don't want him back?"

"Heavens no, my life is calm. I do what I want, when I want. Over time I realized the man's a jerk. One who did me a favor by leaving."

"A jerk?"

"He wanted me to have a face lift. Said he'd loved my pretty young face. Apparently my wrinkles were a personal detriment to him."

"How did you respond?"

"I considered it, but having seen photos of famous women who've had plastic surgery, I felt apprehensive if not downright scared. About half looked beautiful, the others looked like aliens. I wasn't willing to risk the latter."

"Eva, you seem emotionally stable. I don't understand why

you're at a therapist's office."

She tugged her pink suit coat tighter. "For a dose of courage."

"Why courage?"

"This evening is the rehearsal and dinner for our daughter's wedding. I've avoided Ethan for three years. I'll have to sit beside him and his thirty-eight-year old wife. I'm sixty-eight and could be her mother. Actually, she's two years younger than my daughter. He'll have us side by side. Easy to see that leaving the old girl was a good move."

"You're a lovely woman."

"I'm not fishing for compliments, Ms. Simon."

"Accept the fact that you're a gorgeous woman."

"Difficult when my husband drop kicked me to the curb, because of a few wrinkles and sagging breasts. I almost scheduled a facelift three months ago, so I'd look good at the wedding. Ridiculous I know, but…"

"As I've counseled many divorcing women I've found that it's common, regardless of age, for women to want their ex-husbands to regret that they divorced them. A desire for the husband to realize he made a terrible mistake when he left. This even from women, like yourself, who never wanted the men back in their lives."

"Glad to hear I'm not alone, but that won't help me through tonight. Maybe I need a mantra to repeat in my head, or a quick swim in the fountain of youth. Feel silly coming here. I need to get a backbone and face growing old."

I wondered what Mr. Perfect felt about his sags and wrinkles. Somewhere in history some old fart started the rumor that men grow better looking with age, and the myth survived. I was tempted to point this out to Eva. *Unfortunately, sarcasm has no place in therapy.*

When I got out of my head Eva was standing. My silence had sent the wrong message.

"I'm sorry for wasting your time. You see women with big problems, and I'm complaining about wrinkles."

"Wait in the lobby for ten minutes. I have an idea."

"Sure," she said, obviously flustered.

The door closed and I punched in Samuel's number.

"Samuel, my client needs an escort this evening to protect

her from an ex."

"He got a history of abuse?"

"Has a history of being an asshole. She's apprehensive about going single to their daughter's wedding rehearsal dinner. Dreads the comparisons to his young wife. A man beside her might boost her self-confidence. Per hour pay is same as usual. If you're willing I'll get an okay from her, then have her phone you directly to figure out the time line."

"I'll do it. Business slow lately. I'd do anything for a buck."

"I'll get back to you."

"Sure thing."

Eva looked up from a magazine as I seated myself on the lobby sofa.

"I phoned a friend of mine—Samuel. He's a handsome man about your age. He agreed to accompany you tonight. My only dose of courage."

"Oh, no—no escort service. Ethan's young wife would spot that a mile away."

"Samuel is a private detective. I hire him occasionally to help with cases."

"So you pay him?"

"Yes, by the hour, which I'll add to your bill."

She looked doubtful, "You know anything about him?"

"A great guy, and a friend for years. He'll know how to handle your situation discreetly."

Eva shook her head. "Not exactly a self esteem booster to hire a date."

"It's to help you through one evening. I assumed you didn't want a wedding escort."

"I'll be fine at the ceremony. Sitting with my family at the reception."

"What's your answer?"

"I think... yes."

"Here's his number. Call to give him the schedule and dress code. I hope this helps."

"Not sure, but I think it will. Thanks, Marcy."

"You're welcome. I'll phone Samuel with a heads up. He'll be expecting your call."

———◆———

My weary body forced me to bed at 10 p.m., but my brain danced scenarios in my head. Samuel holding a gun to Ethan's head. Someone calling Samuel a bimbo. Samuel drinking too much, and throwing plates at Ethan.

I last viewed the clock at 11 p.m. It read midnight when I woke from a coma like sleep, to the ringing phone.

"Yes," my word stumbled out.

"Sorry, so late Marcy. I thought young'uns partied all night."

I lay flat, my body refusing to sit up. "What's up?"

His words sauntered out. "Wanted to report in. Everything went great. Eva looked twice as good as her ex's made-up arm candy. I'm no psychologist, but Eva seemed happy."

"Super news! How many hours did you work?"

"None."

"Zero?"

"Yep, going with her to the wedding, too."

"Put it on your bill?"

"I should pay you for sending me. Eva is a treasure."

Finally my brain clicked. "Oh, I get it."

"Slow trip," Samuel joked.

"Unfair, I was asleep—brain disengaged."

"I'll give you that."

"So you REALLY like her?"

"I do. Hope she feels the same. Go back to sleep."

I rolled over and stuffed my head in the pillow fluff. *Matchmaker, Matchmaker* played in my head until I fell asleep.

My alarm went off at 7 a.m. I called my work answering service to pick-up messages. Eva's voice requested a call back. Curious, I poked in the number.

"Eva, it's Marcy. Did everything go okay last night?"

Her rhythmic voice danced in my ear. "Fabulous, Samuel's a perfect dear. I ignored Ethan. I'm so grateful. Wanted you to know Samuel is attending the wedding tonight. Be sure and add the time to my bill."

"Samuel called earlier, said there's no charge for either

night. Apparently, he's quite taken with you, Eva."

"Oh my! Who would ever have thought he'd like me, too."

"You feel the same?"

"Absolutely, you're such a blessing Marcy. Thank you so much."

"You're welcome. Have fun tonight."

"I guarantee we will, bye."

"Bye."

I brushed my teeth, and applied make-up thinking about Eva's words. I spoke to my mirror reflection. "Girl, it's been a long time, maybe never, since anyone referred to you as a blessing."

CHAPTER THIRTEEN

FINDING VON

It was time to find Von. My practice wouldn't allow for more than three or four days off. I decided to leave that morning and return home Saturday.

My hastily packed bag clunked as I side swung it into the trunk of my new Camry. Feel more at home in the Mustang, but its age foreshadowed an array of mechanical problems that I don't want to risk on a long trip.

The map showed St. Louis 950 miles away. I planned to drive until my body cried for mercy, then stop for a short night's rest. The weather report looked clear. Hopefully, no storms would erupt.

Miles and miles of pavement, quick pee stops, mediocre food, and a marginal motel tell my journey's tale.

Around 5 p.m. Wednesday I parked in front of a homeless shelter in St Louis. The place sat in a forlorn, forgotten stretch of old buildings left behind when the city spread.

I checked the lock on my car twice, then a third time.

A shallow-eyed man gestured with his pinky finger.

"Hello," I said, as I passed him on the way to the shelter door.

His droopy eyes focused on my expensive bag. "Can you

spare a ten for an old blind man?"

"There isn't one here."

His head shook repetitively. "Take pity on an old man."

"Look like you're under fifty. If I come back in twenty years I'll help you out."

A filthy hand clutched the bottom of my purse. "Need some liquor before my head explodes all over the sidewalk. You'll slip and fall," he warned.

I tugged and swiveled to disengage his grasp. "I'll be careful." I pushed through the door.

The guy slopping food on pink plastic plates was probably in his mid-twenties. A stubbed face and shaved head topped his pudgy body. A wad of black chest hair formed a vee at the neck of his white T-shirt.

An elderly woman reached a plate toward him. "More please."

The guy's nostrils flared. "MOVE ON DOWN."

I waited patiently until the last person passed the grump.

"Excuse me, I have a question."

He snarled as he looked up from the pot he was moving toward the sink.

His eyes caught my face. "What can I do for you, pretty lady? Cause there's plenty I'd like to do."

Hope, the pervert washed his hands before serving the meal.

"Your mood improved. I feared you were going to snap the heads off your diners."

He leaned closer to deliver a smelly whisper. "The low life bums get a handout, then ask for more."

"Thought you were one of them," I said sweetly.

His fist waved in the air. "Cram it girl. Stupid cop stalked me until I made a mistake. Community shit service for driving drunk."

My jaw tightened. "Think of it as an opportunity to enrich your life and theirs."

"Oh crap—a do-gooder. What do you want?"

"I'm looking for a friend—Von Sandburg." I opened my purse to find Von's photo, then realized I'd left it on the passenger seat. "He's six feet, slender, a natural redhead but brunette the last time I saw him. Heard he was spotted under a bridge sometime back."

"I don't keep up with trash, lady. Even if I did wouldn't share with a smartass woman. Screw you. Get lost." His middle finger signaled farewell.

"It's been great." I slammed out the door.

The blind pretender looked up when I stopped in front of his crouched body.

I dug a bill out of my wallet. "Ten for information."

"You got a twenty?"

"First let's see if you can help."

"Ten to listen, another ten if I've got an answer."

My ten now his, I repeated my Von question.

"He could be anywhere," Pretender said.

"May have red hair—gay."

Pretender flattened the bill against his chest, as if he wanted cash close to his heart. "A long haired redhead ate breakfast here couple days back."

"Where might he be now?" I asked.

"Moved on or maybe…"

"Where?"

A gaping mouth exposed Pretender's rotten teeth. "Another ten bucks would lubricate my memory."

Irritation set in, "I'm not the national bank."

"You look like you are. Is that your fancy car?"

"Yes."

"Let's go for a ride. I'll help you track him down. Not good for a lady to travel alone."

The collar of a plaid shirt stuck out from the neck of his scraggly sweater. Next came a tan jacket followed by a blotched and holed leather coat. The sole of his left boot flapped as I followed him to my car.

Done some pretty stupid things in my life, but this may be the last one.

I rolled the window down hoping a gust of wind would neutralize his smell. Also, keep my lunch from ending up on my lap.

"Turn left here, and drive a mile," he directed. "I'm Serge."

"I'm Marcy."

Minutes later he motioned toward a barred-window liquor store. "Back soon." He swayed toward the establishment's door as if his body balanced on a tight rope.

This was my chance to escape. Push the gas and make dust and rocks fly as I speed to safety. Then what? Had no idea where to find Von. Serge's vice appeared to be liquor not sexual perversion. A bet on him seemed preferable to questioning a series of strangers under bridges, and in dark alleys. I imagined that within an hour I'd be chiding my decision. Probably chained in a dark cavern with mice nibbling my toes.

Serge gulped on one bottle, while his left hand clutched a second, as he moved toward my car. Guess it does take some coordination to drink, walk, and clutch.

He flopped into the seat, but didn't spill a drop of booze.

"Where we headed?" I asked with a sideways glance.

He caressed the bottle as if holding a lover. "The sweetness touches my lips and rolls down my throat."

"Does the liquor poet have directions?"

"Make a right then go three miles. You'll see a patch of river. Four lane goes into two."

Serge suckled his bottle like a baby pig as I maneuvered through the unlit streets.

"Whoa," I yipped as his bobbing head lost bottle control.

Too soon to be drunk, but who knew how much he drank before I showed up.

Serge startled and spilled a little of his precious booze on the bottom of his coat.

"NO, NO," he hollered. Pulled the hem up and sucked the liquid.

"Is this the place?" I asked.

"Yep, stop at the street light. We'd walk from there."

I retrieved pepper spray from my purse, and stuffed it and keys in my jeans pocket. I pushed my purse deep under the seat, then locked the doors.

Serge stumbled every few steps, as we tracked forward. Lightning flashed and thunder grumbled in the distance. Poe should've been here—a perfect dark and dreary night.

The underpass loomed ahead. Our path now dotted with hollow-eyed rejects from humanity. A shopping cart overflowed on my right. Close scrutiny revealed a petite woman curled beneath a filthy quilt. One foot latched through the under rail of her cart. A little farther a man's eyes transfixed on my boobs as we walked past.

The homeless were flung about, no order, no civility—stray people, like lost dogs. I assumed a combination of runaways, kicked out, criminals, and hard times.

Raindrops slowly drummed my body. I kept behind Serge as he tromped forward.

Someone had lit a small brush fire under the cover of the bridge. We joined the semicircle around the flames.

"Have any of you seen this man?" I held up Von's photo. The flames lit its surface. My words sounded soft, apprehensive. I expected them to turn on me for disrupting their fire ritual.

One person spit toward the photo. The boob guy moved his mouth like a fish. *How had he caught up so fast?*

A woman with dirt highlighted hair spouted through a toothless mouth, "Don't try to take one of my people or I'll strangle you." She lunged forward, her face coming within five inches of mine.

"Good God, Joan of Arc," Serge yipped, "this little woman ain't going to hurt anyone. You need your meds, gal."

Joan backed down.

Three people glanced briefly at the photo as they passed it around the fire. The fourth tossed it into the flames, with a twisted grin.

Serge mumbled, "You heathens, where's that redheaded queer?"

Liquor must be a power source for my new partner. I should've taken a couple of swallows myself.

"He sleeps in the drain pipe," boob guy answered. "Should wash out soon."

I followed his pointing finger, then bent low to examine the circular cement tunnel that ran under the street. A man lay there. A small amount of water puddled beneath his body. *Could this be Von?*

"Go away," a voice shrilled, "or I'll poke sticks into your eyes."

I knelt at the end of the pipe and leaned in. "Von?"

The man scurried forward, crawling commando style through the pipe. Soon the head of the shrunken body rose from the other side of the street.

A mane of red hair spilled on his shoulders. No shirt

covered the shallow chest. Tight leggings pulled to his waist, and old combat boots were all he wore. He was a human skeleton with a thin layer of flesh covering pointy elbows, and a bulging backbone.

"VON?"

His body slumped to the ground. I ran to him. The rain forced his facial dirt into squiggling lines of mud.

I wrapped my arms around his quivering body. "Von, it's time to go home."

Pain wrenched his face. "Lost my heart. Lost my soul."

Had the stark misery of his life sucked sanity from his brain? What if I was taking a lunatic home?

I pulled him to standing and continued to grasp his hand as we walked past the gathering of lost people. Serge dropped in line behind us.

The storm broke, and hail attacked the car. Lightning threatened to send us into oblivion, and rumbles of thunder escalated my apprehension. Chill bumps covered every inch of my body as I shook in the driver's seat.

Von huddled in the back seat. His eyes caught mine in the rearview mirror, when lightning illuminated the inside of the car. Was his internal light sucked out with his spirit? The sorrow in his eyes burned through the reflection.

Serge sat in the passenger seat caressing his second bottle. The first one was a vague memory. I dropped him off at the homeless shelter then drove thirty miles to find a decent hotel.

I directed Von to stay put, while I checked in. Didn't know if it was safe to share a room, but I couldn't risk him taking off.

After leaving a clean nightgown on the toilet seat. I told Von to wash his hair and shower while I found dinner.

When I returned with fried chicken I found him sitting stiffly, on the bed, in my plaid nightgown. A rubber band pulled his hair back.

I fluffed a pillow and lay against it. He did the same. "You're safe now, Von. We're going to start over." I pressed his hand, and he reciprocated.

"I missed you, Marcy."

"And I you my dear friend. Now we begin again."

"I've lost me," he murmured.

His haunted tone sent chills down my spine.

"We'll bring you back together," I promised. "We're the perfect team."

CHAPTER FOURTEEN

CHEATER'S TEST

As soon as we arrived home Von insisted he was ready to assume the secretarial position. This subject brought up as we lounged in the living room watching a movie.

I tried logic. "It's too soon. You've been to hell. Recovery time is essential. I know—I'm a psychologist, remember?"

Von's jaw tightened. "I must work. Be useful. Don't want to suck off your good will anymore than I have to."

I turned off the television. "I'll agree to you starting work if you begin therapy with Damon. He's a psychologist housed in my office building."

"Something else that costs money. I'll owe you a fortune. I'm doing fine."

"So you're telling me that you don't feel disoriented or depressed?"

Tears clouded his eyes. "Okay. I'll go to Damon. I'm such a burden."

"Enough, Von. Let me confess—I found you for myself. I had no administrative assistant, and no best friend. This is all about me, so forget the thanks. I'll work your tail off, and talk until your ears shrivel."

He smiled, "Glad we cleared that up. I thought I'd turn

into a kept man."

"You're not that lucky."

---◆---

Shopping for Von's new clothes was our first order of business Monday morning. Von's former flamboyant taste now conservative. He selected dark dress slacks and solid button-down dress shirts. His eyes gleamed when he saw a pair of fake alligator dress shoes, which I insisted we purchase. Three T-shirts, six dress shirts, underwear, four slacks, couple pairs of jeans, and one red silk shirt comprised his start-up wardrobe.

Our purchases made he embraced me. "Thanks. How about lunch to celebrate my new job? I'll pay you back out of my first check."

"Unfortunately, I have a luncheon date with Celeste. I'll drop you off at my office. First we'll make a quick stop for you to change clothes."

"What's my assignment?"

"Check out the office. Decide how you want things arranged. If a woman requests an appointment for counseling tell her you'll phone back after 2 p.m."

An hour later I left him at the building entrance with a key and directions. Another thirty minutes and I arrived at Celeste's designated restaurant.

Celeste sat at a corner table between two women. One in a cream-colored suit with an overly ruffled blue silk blouse, overly made up, and as it turned out overbearing. The other woman, slim as a human reed, wore a black jersey dress that skimmed her bulge-less body. One teardrop jade necklace matched earrings that highlighted the upward swirl of blond hair.

I assumed Celeste would be alone. Irritation prickled my brain. My fingertips pressed my temples trying to ease stress.

Celeste stood and pressed my right hand in both of hers. Her new hair color looked like a beanie on her nearly burred head. A red jumpsuit with the added flash of a silver belt and shoes looked a bit tacky for the upscale restaurant.

"Marcy, this is Adrianne Perry." She pointed to the overdone one. "And Leeza Matthews," indicating the thin blonde. "We have a proposition for you." A crackling laugh escaped Celeste's red lips.

Dread crept into my gut. I knew I was the main course at this luncheon.

I forced a smile, and lowered myself into the chair. "What have you gotten me into?"

"We'll order before we discuss," she said.

After the waitress exited, I caught Celeste eyeing me over her glass of white wine.

I met her stare, "What?"

"It's pay up time, Marcy. Remember that favor."

I rubbed the back of my neck. "I'm trying to forget."

"I remember it well."

"I bet."

Adrianne gulped down her shot. Leeza stirred her liquor. *Why are they apprehensive?* "Spit out my fate, Celeste."

"We three have a constant feud that you can solve. A perfect fit, I think, for your side practice." She gave me an annoying wink.

Adrianne nodded in agreement. "These two lambs think their husbands won't cheat. I know better. Every man in the world strays if a pretty young thing with a tight ass tempts him. Can't believe they're so vulnerable, or maybe I should say—stupid."

The conversation paused as the waitress set salads on the table.

Leeza fingered her bread stick. "You don't think there are any faithful men?"

A speck of lettuce adhered to Adrianne's tooth as she responded. "Sure, until temptation offers an alternative. They're all ruled by their cocks."

Celeste curled her lip, and touched her tooth to signal Adrianne.

"What's your stand on this controversy?" My question directed at Celeste.

"Most men will cheat, but none of our husbands are the wayward type. They have steak at home. Our guys don't have to pick up street scraps."

"You're so naïve," Adrianne scoffed.

"We'll find out with Marcy's help," Celeste stated.

"What are you asking me to do?" I took a drink of Diet Coke but wished for a shot or two.

Celeste paused as the waitress topped the water.

She whispered when the waitress turned away. "We want you to test their faithfulness."

I gasped, "Seduce your husbands?"

"No silly," Celeste retorted. "We'll hire that prostitute friend of yours to entice the men. You'll inhabit an adjoining room. Just in case the whore's ego is so big that she won't admit she couldn't convince some guy to screw her. Especially if it's for free. Her self-esteem might bottom out."

Celeste and Adrianne laughed. Leeza studied her salad.

My eyes widened. "Why would I ever agree to this?"

Celeste's gritty tone sizzled. "You owe me."

"This is much more than one favor." Anger seeped into my words. "And ridiculous to boot."

Adrianne piped in, "We'll each donate five hundred to that Women's Shelter that Celeste says you love like a baby."

"Also, a couple of hundred each for Barbee the whore," Celeste added.

First she mentioned my side practice, now Barbee. A flame of angry words erupted from my mouth. "You aren't supposed to tell anyone what I told you during therapy sessions."

Celeste shook her head. "I didn't mention therapy, but you just did. How soon can you start the sex experiment?"

"So I'm in the position of causing three divorces? Not going there."

"Good lord," Adrianne huffed. "Don't be such a prude."

I turned to Leeza, "Do you really want your husband tested?"

Her eyes didn't leave the salad. "I do, Adrianne should admit that she's full of crap, and pay off the bet."

"And you, Celeste, are you that sure of your husband?"

"He's so damn squeaky-boring-clean that I'm going to spend the money this afternoon that Adrianne will owe when she loses the bet."

"Too much pain can result from your experiment. I won't be part of it."

Celeste's shoulders slumped, then straightened. A twinkle

in her green eyes, "You don't have to name who cheated and who didn't. If at least one cheats, Adrianne wins. If none of them cheat, no harm, no foul. They'll all be golden and our marriages stronger."

Adrianne squinted, "What do you say?"

"I require a three thousand dollar check from each of you for the Women's Shelter."

"That's too much, Marcy. Don't rob us."

"Let me point out, Celeste, that you spend that much for clothes on a monthly basis."

"Taking advantage," Adrianne complained.

"I don't want to participate in your experiment." I pushed my chair back. "I'm happy to forget the whole thing."

The two women nodded toward Celeste.

She spoke, "Okay, we'll pay."

"Curiosity is expensive," Adrianne added.

"Write your checks while I'm in the restroom. By the way, how will Barbee end up alone with your husbands?"

"We'll arrange that," Celeste assured me. "You two just show up and administer the cheater's test."

When I returned four checks lay in the center of the table. One made out to me to cash and pay Barbee, and three made out to the Women's Shelter. I stuck the checks in my purse then looked at each woman in turn. "You do understand that I'll never tell which men cheated?"

"Yes," they each said in off-kilter unison.

I left without a goodbye or finishing lunch. No more meetings with these women.

Back in my car, headed toward the shelter, I searched for a pinch of guilt, but found only elation. The shelter struggled to survive on a daily basis. Nine thousand dollars would keep the facility open until after Christmas. Barbee's budget was from one trick to the next—probably didn't make over fifty dollars a john. Six hundred dollars was like a lottery winning.

Good works as a result of a sex experiment may not have been God's work. None-the-less the shelter would receive help, so perhaps there was a little virtue in this nastiness.

Not feeling the floor beneath my feet, I waltzed through the shelter door.

Sonya sat at her desk. She peeked over the top of her glasses.

Strain emphasized the lines on her forehead. "What can I do for you, Marcy?"

"No, what can I do for you?" I tried to contain my smile, but felt the outcome was likely an unattractive smirk.

"Oh, a bag of gold, diamonds, or rubies. The bills have taken over my positive attitude, my desk, and most of my time."

"Your wish is my command." I waved a check in front of her.

She stood, leaned forward, and snatched it from my hand. "Marcy," her voice peaked. "Where did this come from?"

"All from wealthy acquaintances."

"There's more?" She fell back into her chair.

"Nine thousand total, and I'll donate a thousand, then you'll have the ten thousand you need to keep the shelter open the rest of the year."

"Oh, my goodness." She jumped up, and moved around her desk. Her arms circled me in a ferocious hug. "Prayers are answered, and you're the delivering angel."

I felt my face tighten. Sonya had too much appreciation for a woman whose funding project made her the devil's helper as opposed to an angel. Oh well, at the moment it seemed worth damnation.

"Got to get going. I'm meeting Barbee at the restaurant."

"Well... okay."

I sped toward the door hoping I wouldn't confess my sin before I escaped. A wall of muscle grabbed me as I toddled backward.

Zane barked, "Why are you running? I've seen criminals who looked less guilty."

"Good grief! I'm going out the door not robbing a bank. Blame my poor timing and lousy luck that you showed up. Hope I didn't hurt you." I turned to finally make my escape.

"Wait a minute," Sonya ordered.

I froze in the doorway.

Sonya's eyes rested on Zane's sneering face. "I can't go to the ballet next month. Got a presentation at the armory."

"It's your birthday present, Mom."

"They're considering sponsoring us. I'm giving my ticket to Marcy."

Zane's face turned an unbecoming shade of gray, and I

felt mine blaze.

"You two go, and while you're there learn to get along. He'll pick you up at 5 p.m. two weeks from tomorrow, dinner then the ballet. Go meet Barbee."

Zane's officer tone followed me out the door. "Tell Barbee to shut down her business. Two dead prostitutes this week."

What did he care about Barbee? *Suppose he's one of her clients?*

Polluted Zane thoughts occupied my brain as I drove toward the restaurant. We seldom crossed paths, because I avoided him like the plague. Now he showed up to put the finger right where it belonged on my questionable dealings and me. Geez!

Barbee was holding court at the corner booth when I walked into the restaurant. Two men leaned toward her negotiating a twofer.

One guy turned toward me. "I'd pay double for you, babe."

A storm formed across Barbee's face then erupted. "Then you'll pay double for me, shithead. Get lost, turds, I got an important meeting here."

They departed, but their blended odors of grease and beer remained.

"Let's talk in my car, Barbee," I said softly.

Her voice rose, "Do you think you're a damn special agent? Distracted my johns."

"There's a better deal."

"Trying to save me from my sexual perversions again? I don't want rehabilitation." She pulled back her shoulders. "I'm a well-adjusted sex addict, and I'm going to stay that way."

"Gave that up, Barbee. Matter of fact I have a job for you—actually three—two hundred each."

Barbee grinned. "You my pimp?"

"Not how I'd describe it, but yes in a way I am. Let's talk somewhere else."

"Well, girl, glad I won you over," Barbee stood. Her gold dress was cut to the upper thigh. A mesh fabric across her chest showed peek-a-boo boobs. A gold headband pulled back her tricolored hair. Four-inch gold heels clicked across the restaurant floor as she followed me out the door.

Her legs relaxed into a spread-eagle pose as she sat in my passenger seat. "Tell me girl. What's the gig?"

"First, promise you'll keep your mouth shut."

Barbee moved a finger across her lips. "I'm zipped, girl."

"Here's the deal. I have three clients who want their husbands' faithfulness tested. I'll be in an adjoining room to verify whether or not each man has intercourse with you. You get paid whether they do the deed or not."

A teasing grin stretched her lips. "Ain't no man I can't get going."

"Don't force the issue. If he says 'no' more than two times it's over."

"I'll keep working on him."

"Pay attention, Barbee. If you don't follow directions there's no pay. They have to want it, which doesn't include rape."

Her bottom lip protruded, "Okay bitch."

I took a deep breath. "These are upper-class men. You'll dress like a hot little secretary, not a prostitute."

"Not good enough?"

"It's important to look the part. Think of yourself as an actress. You're playing a role."

"I always wanted to be a movie star."

"If you're agreeable we'll head to the mall for a new outfit and hair color."

She smoothed her striped locks.

"I'll pay for your next dye job."

"You're wasting my john time. How much pay for this shopping trip?"

"Fifty, on top of everything else."

"A hundred," she squawked.

"Seventy-five," I shot back. Not that the extra twenty-five mattered, but the woman was getting out of control.

"I suppose, if we get moving."

"By the way, Zane said to warn you about the prostitute murders. Told you to shut your business down. These jobs will bring in some cash. Surely they'll get the killer soon."

"Zane's a sweetie, but he shouldn't worry about little me. My johns don't kill whores."

Considered asking her what was sweet about Zane, but decided I didn't really want to know.

CHAPTER FIFTEEN

SEX EXPERIMENT

The call came in Friday afternoon. Celeste assured me everything was in place. A designated hotel bar where Barbee would seduce her prey. My hotel room had audio, and visual equipment connected to Barbee's sex nest. Celeste's required proof that the deed was done.

I didn't ask for the how, just the when, where, and who.

———◆———

Barbee looked gorgeous sitting at the bar as she waited for Adrianne's husband. A gray-suit jacket lay across the stool beside her. The low-cut blouse showed a bounty of boobs beneath the thin fabric. A man stopped and nervously asked if he could buy her a drink. Her eyes met mine. I shook my head.

"No thanks," she said, "Waiting for someone."

The next guy hung on to the bar edge for support, as his mouth brushed against her ear. "Sweetheart, I finally found you."

Barbee's breathy voice replied, "Well handsome you know I got it."

One word shrilled out, "Barbee!"

She startled, as if she'd completely forgotten our mission.

"Oops," she said to the stranger. "You're not who I thought you were."

"But I could be."

"No drunks for me—move on—I'm a nice girl." Her Cheshire cat grin directed toward me.

Pretty funny, Barbee a nice girl.

The bartender motivated the drunk out the door.

I barely caught a glimpse of the man's face when he sat beside me. The same dimpled smile, brown hair, and crooked nose of the photo in my purse—Adrianne's husband.

I angled toward Barbee, and readied to vacate my stool. The trick was to signal her to take my place.

Her eyes squinted. Her hands went palms up. She didn't have a clue.

I rounded behind him and nodded. She finally understood, and slid onto the empty stool.

"Excuse me," she said. "Is the hotel restaurant any good? I'm from out of town."

His neck strained sideways so he could see the speaker. A smile stretched across his face. "Only ate here once and not impressed. They do, however, have good drinks. May I buy you one or two, lovely lady?"

"Gosh, that'd be great," she gushed.

Her words sounded more like a teenager than a classy secretary. Didn't matter, he was already enamored.

Thirty minutes later his hand pressed against her butt as they walked toward the elevator. Ten minutes later I watched, thanks to the spy camera, as he pulled down her panties and pushed her onto the bed.

His breaths came in short pants, with an occasional wheeze. Perhaps I should've brought an oxygen mask.

All that was visible of Barbee was her legs wrapped around his butt, and two hands pressing against his back. All the proof I needed that Adrianne's husband was indeed a cheat. This could end the contest, but unfortunately wouldn't. The wives would know the cheater because the others weren't set up to play the game yet.

I continued my watch. I'd seen one porn movie, but this

was weird, and a bit boring. He humped, tried to breathe and she kept blurting, "Oh, oh what a man!"

Ten minutes after it started it ended. I listened closely.

"Hey, baby, great sex. Give me an hour, and we'll have another go at it."

"Sorry," Barbee replied sweetly, "my husband is due back in twenty minutes."

"Shit bitch, are you trying to get me killed?"

He struggled into his pants, fumbled his button, skipped his zipper, slipped on dress shoes without socks, grabbed his shirt from the floor, stuck the socks in his pocket, and left.

I knocked on Barbee's door. "He left fast."

"Afraid I'd fall asleep under him. That guy couldn't turn on a light."

I smiled. "Noticed you weren't moving."

"A waste of my sweet pussy. He didn't even pet her. I wanted to charge the loser extra, but figured you'd shit your pants."

"You got that right. Ready to go?"

Barbee didn't attempt to cover her gaping yawn. "For sure."

Celeste phoned in her husband's test site the next day—a different hotel bar. She scheduled him for 8 p.m. drinks. Celeste would phone her husband, and plead a headache, which would leave her man alone for Barbee's seduction. I admit, a good plan.

I punched Barbee's number into my cell. "It's show time, girl."

"I'm busy. Got regulars to service."

"Get unbusy, I already paid you. Everything is set."

"You're one bossy bitch."

"Change your clothes. I'll be there in fifteen minutes."

"Ain't wearing clothes. Can you make it thirty? My john wants to double his fun."

"Tell him your mother is sick."

"You sure as hell are one sick mother."

Twenty minutes later I stopped in front of Barbee's apartment building. Another five and she walked toward my car as if wearing steel boots. A cigarette hung from the corner of her mouth. Lip-gloss too red, eyelids too blue, but her hair and clothes adequate.

"Hello," I said.

Her finger punched the station selector, then raised the sound until it vibrated the windows, and my patience. I turned it down.

Her hand slapped mine, but she left the volume alone.

"Being a whore makes you grouchy."

"Stop trying to do a job on me psycho-psychologist."

"I know you love your work."

"Damn straight."

"Look Barbee, I have to finish this stupid bet. Spend all my time waiting for phone calls."

She scowled out the window.

"How about an extra hundred, after the third guy, if you pretend you're not terminally pissed."

She almost smiled. "For a hundred I can pretend you're not a BB."

"BB?"

"Bossy bitch."

"Ah, we have a deal then?"

"Works for me," she agreed.

I explained the plan as I drove. "This guy's wife is cancelling a date with her husband. He'll have an empty seat saved beside him. We'll know when he hangs up the call at 8 p.m. that it's time for you to take the seat."

Barbee's lips formed a pout. "Hope this guy knows how to treat a pussy."

"I'll get the room keys from the desk, then meet you in the women's restroom."

At 7:55 everything was in place. I sat on a stool. Barbee hung back. I spotted him. His face mirrored disappointment as his ear received a message through his cell phone. I nodded toward Barbee.

Her firm little buttocks scooted onto the stool next to him.

A shot quickly disappeared down his throat. An irritated look scrunched his handsome face.

Barbee spoke first. "What's your name?"

"Deke," he answered.

"Are you okay? Seem upset."

"Disappointed, my wife stood me up."

"I'd never leave a looker like you alone at a bar. Some girl—like me for instance—might take advantage."

"Thanks for the compliment, but I'm married."

Barbee touched his hand. "Variety is the spice of life."

Deke pulled his hand away, and consumed a second shot.

Her hand rested on his thigh. "I'm so lonely, cure me."

Deke stood, "Sorry lady, going home to check on my wife."

He disappeared out the door.

The red in Barbee's face drifted to her neck.

"Let's head home," I said.

I trailed as she rushed out the door.

Sunk into the passenger seat her words pierced out. "Well, I never!"

"Don't take it personally, Barbee. Much to my surprise there's at least one faithful man left in the world."

Barbee huffed, "Well shit, why did I have to meet him?"

———— ◆ ————

"Same setup for Leeza's husband," Celeste announced five days later.

"Glad when this is over," I blurted into the phone.

Her voice teased. "Don't enjoy watching people have sex?"

"Maybe haven't had occasion to."

"Right. Can't believe you're sticking with this 'no tell' crap."

"That's the deal."

"Don't you think my husband looks great naked?"

"No comment."

Celeste's irritated tone spit out her words. "Same set-up and time tomorrow. I'll send you a photo of Leeza's husband—Monty. Meet us at noon on Saturday to give sex experiment results."

"I don't plan on being hungry that day and time. I know you'll attempt to manipulate the truth from me. I'll send you a text at 12:30 Saturday, then the loser or losers can pay off their sex experiment bet."

"Don't be such a drama queen. We aren't a bunch of vultures who'll eat you for lunch."

"I'm not going to chance it."

"Whatever," her last word before the line went dead.

She doesn't deserve Deke. Probably the only faithful man left in the city, and he ended up with a manipulative witch. Perhaps I could make him mine. Wrap my arms around that muscular body, and drag him home. Save him from her.

My prostitute partner answered on the first buzz. "Barbee, I'll pick you up at seven on Friday—our last victim."

"I'll be ready," she strained. Likely a man on top taking her breath away.

———— ◆ ————

When I arrived Friday evening Barbee was subdued. Her previous failure likely weighed on her ego. I'm sure it's difficult for a woman, who seduced men for a living to find one who rejected her.

I held up my cell phone. "This is our victim."

She eyed his photo. "Maybe a normal man?"

I added a little empathy to my tone, "Likely so."

Not sure if Barbee was in hyper gear or the guy had an excess of horny. Regardless, fifteen minutes after she pushed into his side at the bar they left for the elevator.

I downed my drink and sprinted for the next elevator. Upstairs I sat transfixed as they stripped their clothes as if on fire.

Suddenly he turned into a tickle monster. One hand captured her foot while the other slid repetitively over the bottom. Then he went for her underarms, and lastly between her legs. Barbee's tickle frenzy seemed painful.

Fumbling is how I'd describe him. Patting her back, making her squeal in pain as he teethed her boob. Her head popped up when he tried to push it between his legs.

"No way man," she screeched. "You're all red and yucky down there. That thing isn't going in my mouth."

"Just watch," he grunted.

His hands grasped either side of her head pushing her face into his crouch. Monty's gut-wrenching yelp penetrated the walls. Barbee's head rose, and his hands circled her neck.

"You're dead, skank. Nobody bites me and gets away with it."

My fists attacked the wall between our rooms. "THE COPS ARE ON THE WAY."

He untangled and pushed her to the floor.

"You're no better than a filthy whore. Slut, slut, slut," hissed through his lips as he struggled into slacks.

Barbee cowered in the corner.

His hand formed into a gun as he pointed it toward her. "You tell anyone about this and you're dead meat."

"I won't tell."

He jogged out the door.

I waited a couple of minutes then entered. "You okay?"

"Hell no. Crazy pervert about killed me cause I wouldn't suck his nasty cock. I took a big bite out of the monster's thigh. He'll be hurting tonight."

Her red-blotched neck would soon turn to bruises.

"Sorry, I got you into this Barbee. I had no idea."

"Hazard of the profession," she said. "I been hurt plenty of times, but this guy was a whole package of crazy."

A dark thought flashed in my brain. When Barbee disappeared into the bathroom, I stuffed Monty's jockeys into my bag.

CHAPTER SIXTEEN

AFTERMATH

Hugs, kisses and long walks with Deke invaded my thoughts.

"Earth to Marcy. Where are you? You keep drifting off like a lovesick puppy. Whom are you yearning for?"

Von leaned over the back of the sofa where I lounged. I looked at him then stared at my toenails badly in need of a pedicure. "Foolish stuff. Can't get a man out of my mind."

"Someone I know?" His voice trailed as he returned to the kitchen bar where he prepared lunch.

"Celeste's husband."

His voice heaved across the room. "Whoa girl! Based on the stories you've told me I wouldn't tangle with that witch. What's the attraction?"

"You know, Deke turned down intercourse with Barbee."

"Interesting that your fantasy man refused sex."

"My fantasies never include sex." *The rape left me ambivalent to intercourse. I have a personal conflict between physical desire, and feeling like a dirty, damaged woman.*

"So Deke is the perfect man for you, because he turned down sex?"

"I know I'm screwed up. Don't know why he keeps hanging in my thoughts."

"Well, cut him loose. He's married and faithful. You got nothing, girl."

Von handed me a lunch-filled paper plate.

"I guess you're right. A waste of fantasy."

He wiggled his rear into the small space left by my stretched out body. "You never told me how the last sex experiment turned out."

I sat up. "Trying to forget."

"Forget what?"

"Got out of control when Barbee refused to give the guy head."

"Doesn't sound like Barbee."

"Apparently the guy's penis looked infected."

"How'd she get out of it?"

"Bit the shit out of his thigh. He went ballistic—he went for her neck."

"Did you rescue her?"

"I screamed 'cops' and he jetted out leaving behind his underwear."

"I'm sure the hotel has collected plenty over the years."

"I kept his pair."

Von's head jerked. "Was the guy that sexy?"

"Oh lord, no. I got this creepy feeling. When he went from zero to violent in seconds."

"So you kept his underwear?"

"For DNA."

Von shook his head. "Detective Marcy?"

"Don't look at me that way."

"Surely you can admit that collecting underwear for DNA is strange even for you."

"Ha, ha, funny boy. I kept them because Zane said a couple of prostitutes were murdered."

A potato chip dropped from his mouth. "You think this guy's the killer?"

"No idea. We set him up. He didn't solicit Barbee nor did he actually know that she's a prostitute, but he did go berserk."

"Where you taking that underwear?"

"Maybe on my ballet date with Zane next weekend. That should solidify his lowly opinion of me."

Von grinned, "Let me visualize you handing Zane dirty

jockeys at intermission. A shocking outcome."

I caught the time on my cell phone as it buzzed. I'd forgotten—a Freudian slip perhaps—my promised call to Celeste.

"What's the hold up, Marcy? We're waiting for your report."

"Catching up with Von."

Anger tightened her words. "Good grief, you see him every day. What's the result?"

"Adrianne wins. At least one husband cheated."

"Who were the good boys? Or should I say 'boy'?"

"Not the deal," I answered flatly.

Celeste's tone burned my ear. "Get over it, Marcy. Don't be such a pain in the ass. We're dying to know."

"Got to go, Von's wine glass is almost empty." I pushed the red button.

I imagined her ranting and raving to Adrianne and Leeza about my goody-two-shoes proclamation.

"Conversation didn't seem pleasant, and my glass is plenty full," Von pointed out.

"Just needed some exit words. I heard Adrianne and Leeza, in the background, egging her on."

Von's mouth puckered, "Lisa as in L-e-e-z-a?"

"Yes, why?"

"A Leeza scheduled an appointment with you for this Monday at 10 a.m."

Potato chips flew as my plate flipped into the air.

———◆———

Monday came at warp speed, or so it seemed. I heard Leeza's voice in the outer office when she checked in with Von. What did she want? Celeste probably sent her to harass sex experiment results out of me.

I stood when she entered. The white dress she wore blended too well with her pale skin leaving a sickly appearance.

"Before you sit Leeza I want you to know I'm not divulging anything from the sex experiment. Tell Celeste to give it a rest."

She lowered herself into a chair. "She didn't send me."

"Then why are you here?"

"I need to know if Monty acted normal with the prostitute?"

"Does he act normal with you?" I asked.

"He frightens me—sometimes."

"How's that?"

"Demanding." Her hands trembled, "Did he hurt the whore?"

"I'll say it again. I won't reveal what happened in that room."

"I know he screwed her. What I need to know is if he hurt her?"

"If you know he cheats, why did you bet he wouldn't?"

"You know Adrianne and Celeste, no way do I give a hint of my personal life to those cougars."

I clamped my lips. *Was Celeste behind this? Another scheme to get me blabbing.*

Leeza continued, "I'm thinking it's just me he hates."

"You seem very sure that he cheats."

"I found a panty stash in his tool box—bikinis and thongs mostly. Some with dried blood—I imagine horrible things."

Chill bumps covered my arms. "You think he's violent with these women?"

"Probably just me he hates."

"Why are you here, Leeza?"

"I told you, I want to know if he hurt her."

"You women have to lay off. I'm not divulging information. If you're here because you want therapy the answer is no. I'm too personally involved. Check in with the psychologist next door. He'll work with you."

She stared through bagged eyes. Fear tightened her face into a bizarre mask. Her words struggled out. "Am I the only one he hurts?"

My head moved slowly from side to side, activated by empathy not reason.

"Thank you," she said and moved toward the door. She turned back, "I thought there was something wrong with me. Now I know it's him."

The door closed behind her. My head rested on my desktop. Surely there was something I should've said to Leeza. Perhaps "Run, run as fast as you can."

CHAPTER SEVENTEEN

LIFE DESTROYED—OLIVIA

The wheelchair's solemn hum announced Olivia before she wheeled into my office. An attendant slumped near the woman.

"Wait outside," my new client directed.

The helper disappeared out the door.

"I'm Olivia Reynolds," her words clear, but labored. Twice she sucked the oxygen tube that rested in front of her mouth.

"Approximately a year ago a drunk driver ran a red light. He plowed into the driver's side of my car leaving me paralyzed from the neck down."

I had no response.

"I loved to dance and run. I worked at a fine restaurant. A damn good hostess until he destroyed my life. Now my body is dead. Sometimes I think I'd be better off if my brain died too."

I should probably comment, but there's only one thought in my head. I also would've chosen not to have the ability to realize what I'd lost.

She continued, "I'm the victim of Senator Dean Carlson's alcoholism."

Every two or three words she paused, and gulped in air. A hacking cough thundered from her mouth, bringing me to my feet. "I'll get the attendant."

"No," she gurgled.

I repositioned the oxygen tube, and shortly her breathing evened out.

Finally she continued. "Bad timing to end up on the highway after he'd spent the night drinking. If I'd left the restaurant two minutes earlier or later—'if' obviously didn't happen."

"Olivia, the intake sheet didn't give a reason for your counseling request. I assume you want therapy due to emotional trauma?"

"I purposely neglected a reason. I didn't want you to refuse. I heard that you have special services beyond counseling."

I gasped.

"Don't worry, I'm not asking you to put me down like a lame horse, or a broken cat hit by a car."

My breathing returned to normal. "Glad to hear."

"Everyone knows about the senator—front page news," Olivia stated. She took a puff of oxygen, as I nodded—indicating my knowledge of the guy. "Are you also aware that I lost my case against him?"

"How's that possible?"

"The cop 'forgot' to give him the field sobriety test or use the breathalyzer. No doubt he was intimidated by the rich politician."

"But you still should've won, right? He ran a traffic light. Even if he wasn't drunk it was still his fault."

"His friends are judges and attorneys. I'm a paralyzed former hostess with a divorced daughter who has three children under seven. I'm supposed to help her, but look at me now. My money is gone. Lacey, my daughter, can't take care of three children, a full-time job, and me. So I'm bequeathing myself to Carlson, the man that the law wouldn't touch."

"Does your daughter want to help?"

"Trust me, she's a good person, but regardless of what she says I won't burden her."

"What do you want, Olivia?"

"To burden the man who destroyed my life."

"I don't understand, Olivia."

"Leave me with him. I want to call out his name as he walks into work. Placed on his front porch on a rainy day. Left on his driveway, so I can welcome him home from work."

"What do you hope to gain from this experiment?"

Tormented words labored out, "One of two things: he'll kill me or pay to get rid of me."

"The first of those two alternatives sounds ominous."

"Either works. If there's a dead body the legal system might even apply to the senator. Marcy, I don't have money, but your pay off will be substantial if he throws in the towel."

"Not worried about payment. Concerned that he may take legal action against you for homesteading on his lawn."

"That'll put him on the newspaper's front page, where he doesn't want to be. I'm hoping he'll fold, and hand over the cash. We can think of it as our adventure."

Tension drifted from my body. "An adventure like none other."

I returned Olivia's smile as a spasm of coughs took hers away. After a few minutes of recovery she asked me to call her helper. The attendant handed me an envelope.

"That's contact information," Olivia explained, "so you can call my daughter in the event of an emergency. I also have a bank routing number listed so you can handle the transaction if the senator folds." Her cough started and continued as the attendant pushed her through my office lobby and out the door.

Since I didn't feel competent to handle Olivia's adventure alone, I called in Earl and Samuel. Neither of the men complained even though pay was unlikely.

———— ◆ ————

Near 4:30 p.m. that afternoon, we arrived at the senator's mansion. The men unloaded the bulky chair, and situated it on the sidewalk. Samuel placed a listening device on Olivia, so we'd know if she needed help. We promised to come running, but she ordered, "Not unless I'm dying."

Based on Samuel's snooping we knew Carlson arrived home shortly after 5 p.m.

Earl sat in the back of Olivia's old van. I rode shotgun.

"You two didn't need to come," Samuel said.

"Curious, I want to see how it goes, then I won't be so apprehensive if I have to transport her alone."

Earl chimed in, "Curiosity got me, too."

We fell silent as a red Mercedes pulled into the driveway. A tall figure climbed out, slammed the car door, and ran toward Olivia. His head turned scanning the fronts of neighboring houses.

"What are you doing here?" A stiff voice barked through our eavesdropping device.

Olivia's words came out even and calm. "Looking over your lovely home. I'll lose mine soon. Broke and can't work, but you already know that, don't you?"

"I won the case—exonerated."

Her tone strengthened. "You're telling me?"

"What's wrong with you?"

"Perhaps the crash also affected my reasoning ability."

"Get out of here before the neighbors see you," he hissed.

"How am I supposed to leave?" Olivia croaked.

He pointed a finger at her face. "Same way you came."

"Friends are gone. Told them I wanted some alone time with you," she heaved.

My heartbeat increased.

"I'll call a cab." His anger seemed dampened by the woman's struggle to speak.

She gradually got the words hacked out. "How do you propose to put this wheelchair in a cab?"

"Then I'll call an ambulance. You sound like you're going to die on my lawn. I've suffered enough. Trial almost ruined my career."

Olivia's laughter came out as a long croak. "Look who's talking about a ruined career. You're quite the joke."

"It was an accident. I can't change that. It is what it is. No reason to destroy both our lives."

"I want you to hurt, too," she said softly.

"I've suffered plenty," he jabbed.

"And you destroyed my life."

His anger-saturated words blasted, "That's what fate dealt you so face it."

Earl's disgust rang from the back seat, "Bastard." The flesh around his fake eye changed from dull red to bright.

I swallowed a little vomit that pushed into my throat. Samuel gripped the steering wheel.

"I'm calling the police," Carlson spouted.

"Good," Olivia croaked, "With the police come the reporters."

"You're trespassing."

"Not nearly as bad as driving drunk."

"DAMN YOU." He crammed his body back in his Mercedes and gassed it into the garage. He left barely enough time for the automatic door to go up without taking the roof off the car.

Five minutes later Olivia's voice signaled. "Give me another few minutes. I figure he's inside drowning any conscience he has left."

After awhile Samuel drove the van to the curb. I surveyed the exterior of the mansion. No sign of Carlson peeking out a window.

Settled inside the van, Olivia's breathing evened. "How did I do team?"

"You put his life in danger," Samuel answered. "Thought Earl was going to kill the jerk."

I turned to make eye contact with her. "I thought you did well, Olivia. Stayed calm, which is important when dealing with an explosive person."

"What's next?" Samuel asked.

"I want to beat Carlson to his election headquarters tomorrow morning."

"Supposed to rain," Samuel informed.

"My mission must continue. Think of me as a quadriplegic super hero."

A few seconds passed before the three of us joined in her laughter.

Later we unloaded at her house. The aid came to meet us.

"I thought you couldn't afford to pay her," I said.

"She agreed to stay for free until she found another job," Olivia answered.

Earl helped the attendant unload the wheelchair, and get Olivia back inside her living room.

The task completed Samuel drove his old Chevy toward Dinah's diner, our rendezvous location.

"What do you guys think?" I held my body stiff, only moving my head, imagining what it's like for someone in Olivia's condition.

"Senator's a tough nut to crack," Samuel answered. "An alcoholic under duress. No telling what he'll do."

Earl's words shot from the back seat. "I'll beat the shit out of him. Threaten to kill him if he doesn't pay."

"Whoa, that's a big jump. Olivia wants money, not murder."

"He deserves to die," Samuel added. "What a piece of trash!"

A Supremes song saturated the air coming from the diner. Dinah had turned up the jukebox. None of us were in the mood, so we didn't go inside.

Earl and I continued our conversation at Samuel's truck window.

"Whose taking watch tomorrow?" Earl asked.

"I'd like to come with, but don't think I can handle the van without one of you," I said.

Samuel's inquiring look sunk into Earl's eyes. "Can you take it? I'm tracking a woman who wanders toward a motel every time her husband leaves for work."

"I'm in," Earl agreed as he squeezed my shoulder. "Breakfast here at six then pick up Olivia."

"That'll work. Night guys." I felt the warmth from Earl's touch as I dragged myself to the Mustang, and made my tired path home.

———◆———

The next morning I found Earl seated at his usual booth. "Sorry I'm late."

"You're looking tired, Marcy."

"Nightmare that I couldn't move my arms or legs. When I woke couldn't go back to sleep for thinking about Olivia."

"Hard life," he acknowledged.

"It's too late for me to eat, not hungry anyway."

Earl stretched as he uncurled from the booth. "We're out

of here."

Soon we were loading Olivia into her vehicle.

I twisted around to talk. "You look pale."

Olivia's mouth turned up slightly. "Not much of a super hero when sitting in a chair on a sidewalk wears me out."

"It was more than that," I corrected. "You faced your nemesis, which takes a lot out of anyone."

"I suppose."

Earl glanced in the rear view mirror. "What's the plan?"

A long gasp struggled out. "Arrive before he shows at his headquarters. Plan to greet him, and scare him into thinking I'll be there when the public arrives."

"He'll be afraid of the negative publicity," Earl concluded.

"Exactly, but that isn't the last card I plan to play. This evening I'll station myself back in his driveway."

We struggled the chair out the van door, and down the wobbling ramp.

Olivia's puff activated the chair down the sidewalk to her station at the bottom of the office entrance steps. Less than ten minutes later the senator parked his vehicle. The camera picked up facial rage as he stomped toward Olivia.

"Get out of here! This is my property," he shouted.

"I'm here to volunteer for your campaign. Need someone to walk the neighborhoods? How about make some flyers?"

"You're mentally ill," the senator stated.

"That's the only disability I don't have."

"What do you want from me?"

"A million dollars for my life. You took it, so pay the price."

"No way are you blackmailing me. I won the case. I'm innocent under the law."

"And you think I'm the one who's crazy. You lied."

"That's your opinion."

"That night, when I lay crushed in my car, you leaned over and cried out that you were sorry. Your liquor breath is my only vivid memory from the wreck."

"No proof."

"Did you pay off that young officer? The one who didn't use the breathalyzer."

"He forgot."

"Star struck, don't you think? Didn't want to tell a hotshot senator what to do."

"My good fortune," he said abruptly.

"Have you stopped driving drunk since you almost killed me?"

"None of your business what I do." Halfway up the steps he turned back. "Don't waste your breath, lady. It'll be a cold day in hell before extortion works on me."

Back in the van, Olivia was unable to speak. When we wheeled her into her living room she managed a raspy, "Tonight."

"Thank goodness her attendant's still there." I said to Earl as he eased his truck into the street.

"Not sure what we're doing, Marcy. This guy doesn't budge one iota."

"I know. He thinks he's immune to repercussions."

"She either gets money to survive, or she'll die trying," Earl speculated.

"I fear the 'die' part is accurate."

"Then we need to pull out," Earl stated.

"Desert her? I can't go there—yet. Let's take her to Dinah's, before we go to Carlson's tonight, and talk her out of this mission."

Earl agreed, "It's a plan."

Back at my office two cancellations gave me a reprieve. I pulled books off my shelf looking for information on the psychological impact of paralysis.

Earl was likely right—I needed to confront problems that there was hope of solving. *But how could I desert her?*

———————◆———————

All eyes turned as Earl pushed Olivia's clunky transportation through the restaurant door. Most patrons continued to stare as I pushed a chair aside so she could park square at the table.

"Cute place," Olivia said.

"Thanks," Dinah answered. "What you folks ordering?"

"Chocolate shake for me," Olivia responded.

"Ditto," I said.

"Usual, Earl?"

"Yep."

The Temptations sang from the jukebox. Olivia joined in as long as her breath lasted.

Maybe not the best time to bring up a problem—when the opposition is struggling to get her breath—but time was short. I took a sip of my shake before I started. "Here's the deal, Olivia, this isn't working. He's not softening, he's hardening."

"It's my only hope."

"The strain is bad for you. If he writes a check he's admitting guilt."

Earl added, "Not likely."

I didn't look at her face as I spoke. "We'll follow through tonight, but we can't continue. You're not strong enough."

Her next words smug, "You're a smart woman, Marcy, you'll figure out how to help me. Let's go."

Olivia's eyes stared straight ahead, and she didn't speak during our trip. Her silence continued as we situated her chair on the edge of the driveway. I knew she was angry, but I wouldn't agree to continue with her plan.

Around 6 p.m. I watched Carlson's vehicle snake around the curve toward his house. As his car darted into the driveway Olivia blew into her sip-and-puff device. The crunch of metal filled the air as his Mercedes crushed the wheelchair.

I stumbled from the van and yelled to Earl. "Phone an ambulance and be ready to take off." I leaned over Olivia— no facial movement, no pulse.

Carlson struggled out the passenger side of his Mercedes, hands waving, his voice blasting. "You saw her, she purposely jumped in front of me." He grabbed my shoulders. "It's her fault. You saw her."

"She's quadriplegic. You're saying that she jumped in front of your car?"

"Rolled not jumped," he corrected. "You've got to tell the truth."

"You suddenly value honesty—interesting turn of events."

"Please," Carlson begged. "You know it was an accident."

"Seemed like you gunned the engine when you hit the driveway."

His fist pounded his chest. "No, no, no—they'll send me to prison."

"Where you belong… unless."

"Unless what?"

"Olivia deserves a nice funeral, and her daughter needs financial assistance."

Anger bubbled up through his fear. "You're blackmailing me?"

"You owe this family. Pay or go to prison. Either way works for me." I heard a siren in the distance. "Got to go before the cops show. Transfer money to her daughter. Make it generous if you want your witness to show." I handed him the envelope Olivia had given me during our first visit.

Carlson's fingers forced his hair into spikes. He raged above Olivia's body crushed against his front tire.

The ambulance and police were coming around the corner when Earl pulled the van away from the scene.

Earl strained out his words, "You think this was her plan all along?"

"I think it was her alternative. Get the cash or die trying. Perhaps my quitting gave her no alternative, but to die sooner rather than later."

"Carlson can't get out of this one," Earl concluded.

"Unless we let him off."

"Will we?"

"I might come forward for the futures of Olivia's daughter and grandchildren."

"This will ruin the guy," Earl speculated.

"Another skin shedding for the snake. Likely he'll recover after the bad publicity dies down. If he cooperates I'll be his witness."

"So you made an offer?"

"I did."

————◆————

Unable to sleep, I tossed and turned. I finally got up and read the senator's story on the Internet. In the news clip Carlson raved about a witness. A detective made a plea for the witness to come forward. The senator said Olivia harassed him, and was at his house the day before. The reporter indicated the senator was charged with negligent homicide.

Throwing accusations at a handicapped woman made Carlson look like the biggest asshole in the world.

I phoned Olivia's daughter at 4 p.m. I started to explain who I was but her mom had already told her about me.

Lacey's voice trembled, "Have you heard?"

"Yes, I'm sorry.

"Mom wanted to die."

"Pull up your bank account online," I said. "See if there's a deposit."

I chewed my thumbnail while I waited.

"My God—half million dollars. Where did it come from?"

"A gift from your mother. She motivated Carlson to do the right thing."

"By dying?"

"It was her choice. Olivia loved you and your children more than anything. Use the money to honor her, and to make a good life for your kids."

"I will," choked out.

I lounged, on the sofa, for a couple of hours before I phoned the police station.

"May I speak to the detective investigating the Carlson case?"

"He's busy."

"Probably looking for me. I'm the senator's witness."

The operator's words blurted. "I'll transfer your call.

CHAPTER EIGHTEEN

STALKING PEGGY

"I'm out of here," I called and grasped the doorknob.

Von's eyes diverted from the television. "Don't you get tired of spending every Saturday morning at the Women's Shelter?"

"These women can't afford services anywhere else."

"Go for it, girl. I prefer my special *Sponge Bob* time."

"You and your cartoons!"

"They keep me sane."

"Later."

Von gave a salute then continued his cartoon ritual.

The breeze tickled my face, while the sun danced shadows around me—a lovely day to walk to the shelter. Footsteps sounded behind me, closing in. My gait doubled in quickness, and I felt a film of sweat surface on my chest. The noise changed from walking to running feet. I swirled. A teen ran past.

Didn't take a degree to figure out my issue. I'd read the intake on Peggy, my newest client. She described her existence as constant vigilance, alertness. Always looking behind searching for her ex-husband turned stalker. He filled her days and nights with terror. Knowing at any point he could grab her and do whatever his twisted mind dictated.

Her words embedded in my psyche, putting me in a state of alertness. Her state, on the other hand, was constant fear.

A combination of raspy sobs and low screeches assaulted my ears as I entered the shelter. Sonya leaned over the sofa comforting a thin woman who lay face down in a throw pillow.

Sonya's head swayed from side to side.

"Peggy?" I asked.

The woman's head rose. Her blond, raven-striped hair was a dirty mane that touched the shoulders of a faded blue shirt. She sniffled, "Yes."

"Come let's go in my office." Gently I pulled her forward not disturbing the pillow she now had clasped to her belly.

"I'll bring Peggy coffee," Sonya offered.

"I don't like coffee."

"Tea?" I asked.

"With sugar."

"Tea with sugar," I called to Sonya.

Peggy flopped on the sofa. The pillow now stuck between her knees.

I rolled the desk chair across from her, and looked into the thick glasses that magnified her bloodshot eyes.

"I read your case file, Peggy. Let's develop a plan to keep you safe."

"I can't do nothing about him. Saw him twice today. Saw him sneak from the cellar this morning when I looked out the kitchen window. He was following me here, but I kept turning left until I lost him."

"Has he hurt you physically?"

She punched the air. "All the time slugging me. He kicked me when I was pregnant." Her foot swung forward.

"You have a child?"

"Lost the baby. Now I can't have any kids cause of him. Told him to get his ass gone. Told me I'd be rid of him on the day he killed me."

"You filed a police report?"

"They don't investigate 'til you're dead."

"Restraining order?"

"I phoned the cops, but he always disappeared before they showed up. It's like he put a bug in my phone."

Sonya set her drink on the table.

Peggy took a sip. "Not sweet enough."

Sonya dropped extra sugar packets on the table and grimaced as she turned to exit. *Wonder what's up with her?*

"Peggy, tell me about your parents."

"Mom's a witch and Dad even meaner."

"Siblings?"

"What's that?"

"Do you have brothers or sisters?"

"Sister took off years ago. Thought she was better than the rest of us. Fool brother drank himself to death."

"Many problems in your life."

"Nothing but. At least once a week Tom hollers from a car window that I better take him back or else." Her finger pointed toward my face. "You and I both know what 'or else' means."

"Are you ill, Peggy?"

Her right hand curled into a fist. "Are you saying I'm sick in the head?"

"No, I'm saying you're too thin and frail. Have you seen a doctor?"

"Can't afford a doctor. They've never done me any good anyhow."

"Did you go to the emergency room when Tom hurt you?"

"Hell no. Don't want folks nosing in my business."

"Some women move to another town to start a new life. Is that a possibility for you?"

"He ain't chasing me off. This is my home."

I kept my tone calm, even. "Do you have neighbors who look out for you?"

"Bunch of whores and pimps, waste of the air they breathe."

I ignored her belligerence. "No family you can visit?"

Spit sprinkled out with her proclamation. "They're all full of shit."

"What I hear you saying is that you must help yourself."

Disgust distorted her face. "You're supposed to help me. You're the head doctor."

"What do you think the head doctor should do?"

"Get him locked in the loony bin, before he kills me."

"You're my patient, not him."

Her nostrils flared, "Duh."

A clump of anger formed in my chest. It was necessary for this session to end before my indignation became evident. I forced my tone to softness. "Our meeting is over. I'll see you at the same time next week."

Hoarse groans hacked out as Peggy trailed toward the exit. "Don't know what to do. Bastard's goin' to kill me dead, and you'll do nothing to stop him."

I locked the front door behind her, without farewell.

Sonya leaned against her office doorframe.

"It appears this woman rubs you the wrong way," I surmised.

"She used to show up once or twice a week until she got pissed. We didn't shower her with enough sympathy and empathy. I think she wanted us to track down the guy and kill him to put her out of misery."

"Maybe she's emotionally disturbed from constantly living in fear."

"Perhaps." Sonya turned away.

I sat on a bench, outside the shelter, pushing in a phone number.

"Samuel, it's Marcy. Have a job for you. My client's ex-husband is harassing her. I need to know what he's up to."

"Can do."

"Peggy doesn't know I'm hiring someone to stalk her stalker."

"Is there a reason for that?"

"She's got a history of drama. To put it bluntly—she seemed unstable."

"Am I looking for anything specific?"

"No, just general information. I wonder if the situation is as big as she lets on or if she's emotionally escalating." I gave him contact info on Peggy.

"May take a while. "

"She's scheduled back next Saturday."

"That's doable. I'll get back to you before then."

"Thanks."

CHAPTER NINETEEN

BALLET

Back at home, I found a note that indicated Von went grocery shopping.

I shuffled clothes in my closet looking for the correct apparel for my ballet date with Zane. He'd left a message two days ago cancelling dinner because he had to work late—like I'd believe that excuse. Anyway, we'd meet at the theatre. The changes were fine with me, though a little disconcerting that someone found me too obnoxious to travel in their vehicle.

Oh well, I'd enjoy the ballet and pretend Deke or Earl was my date. That shouldn't be difficult because I never looked Zane in the face.

I studied my final apparel choices lined up on the bed. The red lace seemed brazen, the white silk too angelic, and the black foreboding. The black it was!

Six hours later Von zipped the back of my bad mood dress. "I think you should wear the red. You know, 'Devil with the red dress on.'"

I playfully pinched his cheek. "Thanks for confirming Zane's opinion of me."

"Now princess, don't be mad, I'm joking."

"Why am I nervous? Like a teenager's first date."

Von circled his finger around his ear. "Psychologist, analyze thyself."

"It's like Zane can see inside my head. Somehow he knows when I'm up to something."

Von chimed in, "Perhaps he's a guilt magnet."

"You joke, but I believe it."

Von flattened out on my bed. "Are you taking the jockeys with you?"

"Can't decide. Probably will wrap them in plastic, and stuff in my bag just in case the opportunity arises."

Von laughed, "Not sure what the opportunity to share dirty underwear looks like. I can drop you off if you want. That would force him to drive you home, and give you a chance to discuss underwear."

"Good idea, but I might risk even more distain. He could leave me in the traffic."

Von rolled off the bed, spread his arms, and flew around the bedroom. "If so I'll fly to your rescue."

"That'd be great. Parking is such a pain."

Von bowed, "Put on your glass slippers, Cinderella, and I'll take you to the ball."

An hour later I stood in the theatre lobby, ticketless, waiting for Zane. Wish I'd thought to get the ticket beforehand. If he didn't show, no ballet, and no ride home.

Von said I looked terrific. He insisted on silver shoes and hoop earrings to interrupt the darkness of my dress. Seemed to work since a couple of men eyed me with appreciation.

A hand touched my shoulder. "Are you alone, Marcy?"

I responded to Celeste, "No, waiting for a friend."

"This is my husband, Deke. Honey, this is Marcy Simon—a colleague."

His arm stretched forward with a flat hand—a human stop sign. "No, not another shrink."

"Yes," I grinned, "another one of those people."

He touched my hand for just a second and my heartbeat escalated.

Deke's perfect white smile lit his face. "Glad to meet you, I guess, even though psychologists are a weird lot."

"Thanks," my voice sang.

"You look familiar," he said.

My words stumbled out, "We've never met."

"Where was it?" He pondered. "Drives me crazy when I can't remember."

Celeste, who looked a bit pale, wrapped a comforting arm around his shoulder.

"It's okay old guy. The memory is the first thing to go."

"Aren't you a supportive old gal?"

"You know it handsome, but better drop the 'old' if you want any tonight."

He rubbed her back. "Yes, baby."

"There he is!" I said too loudly.

Celeste's eyes brightened. "The Italian stallion? You must've won the lottery!"

He swaggered toward me with the usual scorn in his expression.

"Deke and Celeste, this is Zane Scarlatti."

Zane shook Deke's hand, "Pleasure to meet you. We better get seated, Marcy. They shut the doors when the curtain goes up."

Deke's finger pointed toward my face. "I know where I saw you—the hotel bar on Sixth Street. You made eye contact with the little gal who tried to pick me up."

A frown formed on Celeste's face. "Watch that ego, honey. That gal probably wanted a free drink, not a piece of you. Speaking of drinks, let's get one." She turned to me, "Good evening."

Celeste swirled Deke around before I could say goodbye.

"You and Celeste obviously have a secret." Zane accused me as we walked toward the auditorium.

"Yep, she thinks you're an Italian stallion. I corrected her since you're more like a mule."

"Thanks, precious," he snapped.

"You're welcome, sweetheart." If sarcasm were liquid, the floor would've been wet.

His hand rested in the small of my back as he guided me toward our seats. "By the way, may I have a ride home? Von took my car."

"He has his own vehicle."

"Yes, officer, but I didn't feel like fighting the traffic tonight."

His warm breath tickled my ear. "Will it fulfill a dream if I take you home with me?"

My hands clenched. "No, thanks."

"Oh well, a missed opportunity that you may live to regret."

I leaned my face two inches from his. "Not likely."

The curtain went up and the dancing commenced. I glanced at his face. He seemed to enjoy the ballet. Zane was hardcore macho with a capital M. I wouldn't ever have guessed him to be a ballet fan.

At intermission we sat silently until I finally figured out some polite conversation. "I didn't pick up a program. What is the show called?"

"*Balanchine and Beyond*, a ballet in three parts. We just watched *Classical Symphony*, which is my preference of the three."

"It was wonderful. Do you attend the ballet frequently?"

His voice lowered, "Is there an innuendo in your question?"

"Just attempting to make conversation, sorry if I hit a nerve."

"Mom took me to *The Nutcracker* when I was four—the start of her campaign to civilize me."

I couldn't resist, "Sorry that didn't work out."

"In our case, Marcy, silence isn't only golden, it's necessary."

One way to tell me to shut up! Guess I asked for it.

The lights blinked, and my mind strayed from crabby Zane to Part II, *there, below*, my favorite performance of the three.

I saw Celeste and Deke after the show. One glance at me and she maneuvered him in the opposite direction.

Zane grabbed my hand as he led me toward the parking lot. The handholding ended quickly, but felt nice while it lasted.

"We'll sit here until the traffic thins," he said. "What's that smell?"

"Probably my perfume. I have my own concoction, mix two scents together to achieve my own fragrance. Do you like it?"

"Pleasant in a weird way."

Silence filled the car interior. *My opportunity?*

"I told Barbee about the murdered prostitutes. She said not to worry 'cause her johns don't kill no whores.' Also, she said that you're a sweetie."

"Is there a question in that last statement?"

"None of my business," I answered.

"Damn straight."

"Has the killer been caught?"

Zane loosened his necktie. "No, and another woman was killed last night. We found DNA, but there's no match in the system. The killer doesn't have a record. Could be anyone."

I turned my head toward him, and waited for eye contact. "If I give you something, will you keep me out of the legal process?" My words hung in the dark car.

His brows furrowed, "What are you talking about, Marcy? You know something about the killer?"

My hand massaged my forehead. "Probably not, but just in case I thought I should tell someone. The guy went ballistic in seconds with Barbee. I thought he was going to strangle her when she refused oral sex."

The streetlight illuminated his severe expression. "You watched Barbee have sex?"

"This is confidential—I could lose my license."

"Is it that Deke guy? You and Barbee obviously had something going with him, that's why he recognized you. Didn't take you for a pimp."

"Give it a rest, Mr. Holier-Than-Thou. Unlike you, Deke didn't have sex with Barbee."

The cop persona returned. "Where's the evidence?"

"Will you keep me out of the investigation?"

"I'm not covering your ass," he growled.

Enmity churned in my chest. "We're finished then. I'm not playing Russian roulette with my career, my life."

His hand clutched my upper arm. "You're taking the chance that this guy may murder someone else?"

I whipped my arm from his grasp. "Same chance you're taking by not agreeing to my terms."

"You're a manipulative little shrew."

"And you're a giant asshole," I countered.

I swung the door open and jogged toward a cab. My hands

waved wildly, signaling my overwhelming urgency to escape from Zane, my morality judge, and my own conscience.

CHAPTER TWENTY

ADRIANNE AGAIN

Monday started what should've been an uneventful week. Women thinking about divorces, women not wanting divorces that their husbands wanted, women who wanted to strangle in-laws, women overwhelmed by their children, etc., etc. A regular set of problems that pushed my week ahead to Friday. Thankfully, there were only three clients left before the weekend. The first, the mother of Chloe, the little girl I'd observed and developmentally tested at school Tuesday morning. It was to be my first meeting with Chloe's mom, Anne.

Von escorted the woman into my office.

I scrambled to my feet. "Adrianne, what are you doing here?"

"Chloe's school sent me."

"Why did you put a fake name on Chloe's intake form?"

"Leeza said you wouldn't see me. The school referred Chloe. They recommended you, so don't blame me."

I motioned her to sit and did the same.

Overdone as usual, Adrianne wore a too short red dress, expensive boots, and enough diamonds to warrant a guard.

"What's in your hand, Adrianne?"

She held up a photo.

"A new picture of my older daughter, Jordan. I'm so proud of her—so pretty and bright. I wanted you to see that I have a normal child."

"She's cute," I responded. "Do you have a new photo of Chloe?"

"No." Adrianne twisted the diamond stud in her right ear.

"Why is that?"

Adrianne sat straight, her red lips puckered. "She wasn't with us at the time."

"When did you last have photos taken of Chloe?"

"I don't remember."

"Have you ever taken Chloe to a photographer?"

Her eyes flared. "You know what she looks like—a weird kid."

My temper rose, but I kept my words flat. "You're ashamed of her?"

"She's a misfit in my family. Surely, you saw that when you tested her."

"Did you have a tough pregnancy?"

"The worst."

"A planned pregnancy?"

"I didn't want another child. My husband insisted he had to have a son. I was already mad about the havoc the pregnancy wreaked on my schedule and body. You can imagine how hard it was to face having another girl. That meant pressure to have a third child to get his son."

"Did you drink throughout the pregnancy?"

"I always have a drink or two with lunch and dinner. Liquor dulled my disappointment after I found out it wasn't a boy. Try to imagine holding something you don't want in your body for six more months."

"Did your doctor discuss alcohol use during pregnancy?"

"Warned me about numerous things. I'm a rebel. No one tells me what to do."

"Does Chloe have behavioral problems at home?"

"Always. Have to give her directions one at a time and then repeat them over and over. She refuses to pay attention. Her sister says she's lost in space, which fits Chloe perfectly."

I opened the test booklet to explain what Chloe had accomplished and the concepts causing her difficulty. Halfway through Adrianne stopped me.

"I've got errands to run and dinner guests tonight. Give me the bottom line."

She asked for it, making me more than happy to deliver with both barrels. "Based on Chloe's behavior, facial anomalies, low test scores, and your report of alcohol use in pregnancy I have diagnosed your child with fetal alcohol syndrome."

"What does that mean?"

"It means that Chloe is brain damaged as a result of your alcohol use during pregnancy. You should be ashamed of yourself, not Chloe. The 'weird' facial characteristics, the uncontrolled behaviors, and the learning problems are the result of your neglect. You gave Chloe more maternal traits than Jordan will ever have. Therefore, you can take more credit for your so-called 'weird' child than your 'pretty' child. My advice is to love Chloe and care for her every day for the rest of your life. You took away the future she deserved."

Adrianne's gaze dropped to the floor. Her lips quivered, her mouth opened, but no words came out. Silently, she moved from the chair and walked out the door.

I glanced down at her diamond earring stuck in the carpet. Hopefully, expensive things would lose their priority in Adrianne's life.

CHAPTER TWENTY-ONE

FINDERS KEEPERS—BLANCHE

Von called me into the waiting room to meet my next client. A dour-faced woman towered over a petite, white-haired lady.

"I'm Carla Denny," dour-faced announced in an authoritarian tone. "I referred my grandmother, Blanche Selve, for psychological services. I'd like to consult with you alone before your evaluation of Grandmother."

"Is that okay, Blanche?" I asked.

A slight smile indicated agreement.

"You sit in that chair, Grandmother. I'll be right back."

The office door shut behind us. Carla sat stiffly across from me.

"My grandmother is mentally unstable. I fear she'll squander her fortune. She's eighty-two and dementia has set in."

"Give me an example of her lack of stability."

"She planned an Easter egg hunt for me and my two siblings. After the hunt she based our inheritances on notes inside plastic eggs."

I fingered my pen. "Do you have other examples?"

Carla's posture stiffened. "That's enough proof she's mentally incompetent. Your confirmation of her lack of reasoning ability is required for me to legally take over the family finances. After you meet with her give me a report stating that she's incompetent to handle her own affairs. I'll pay you double if the report is ready tomorrow."

A touch of sarcasm seeped into my words. "Why the rush?"

Carla's tone hardened. "She has cancer. If she dies suddenly I'll be left with an estate mess."

"I understand. Please send her in, and I'll start my evaluation process."

I pulled two forms from my desk drawer. The cognistat (a dementia screening test), and a mini-mental status questionnaire would be used in the evaluation of Blanche's mental competency during the course of our conversation.

Blanche rolled her walker into my office, and backed into the chair before sitting gingerly. She patted and fluffed her short white curls. Wrinkles didn't distract from the soft beauty of her face or the concern in her eyes.

Carla hovered beside her.

"Carla," I said firmly. "My session with Blanche is private."

"I… I fear she won't be able to answer your questions."

"If not, I'll consult with you at the session's end."

Carla's chin jerked upward as her mouth twisted into a foul form. Three-inch heels clicked furiously as she stormed out.

Blanche's brown eyes brightened.

"Do you understand why you're here, Blanche?"

"My granddaughter thinks I'm crazy as a bed bug."

"What do you think?"

"Not real sure. Sometimes I go in the same room three times before I remember why I'm there. Have trouble remembering names."

"Do you ever forget where you are?"

"Mostly at home so don't have to worry."

I made sure I covered the information in the screening test and on the questionnaire before returning to our conversation. "Do you handle your own financial dealings?"

"I make the decisions. I have an accountant who carries them out."

"Carla seemed very concerned about your Easter behavior."

"Yes, it really fried her fanny."

"Do you mind telling me the story?"

"Fine with me. I imagine Carla told you that I have cancer?"

"She mentioned it."

"Before my life ends I needed to update my will. I'm a very rich woman. Although, Carla assures me that no one can tell from my off-the-rack clothes. Right before Easter I decided to get my ducks in a row. I love all three of my grandchildren and didn't want to appear to play favorites. I developed a plan to divide my estate. I asked them to visit my home Easter Sunday for an egg hunt and to discuss my will."

She paused and dug in her purse. A photo of three children with Easter baskets eventually ended up in my hand.

"Rob, Carla, and Katie," she announced.

"Cute kids," I responded.

"They did so love my egg hunts." Her eyes appeared to see distant children. "The servants hid the eggs every Easter morning. My grandkids joined most of the town children for the hunt. The hundreds of eggs hidden contained candy, quarters, or tiny toys. My favorite time of the year."

"That sounds special," I inserted.

"Oh, it was. All the kids giggling, running, and happy over the little prizes. Each child was a joy to behold."

"What happened this last Easter?" I questioned to get Blanche back on track.

"This past Easter, after church and dinner, I gathered my three grandkids on my porch. Rob and Katie both brought Easter baskets, as I requested. Those two challenged each other to find the most eggs. Carla called me back in the house for a private chat. She told me there was no way she'd make a fool of herself. Went on to say that she wasn't a child, and it'd be a cold day in hell before she ran around in the bushes carrying a big bowed basket. I told Carla it was her choice."

"I imagine she hurt your feelings."

"Carla ignored my last request. I'd always been there for her, but she refused to help me relive the happiest time of my life. Katie and Rob had a great time. I laughed more that day than my last five years combined."

She took a gulp of the water I handed her.

"I told Rob and Katie to bring their Easter baskets to the dining room table. By then my attorney arrived. As the pair opened each egg they found a small slip of paper that named a specific asset that he or she would inherit at my death."

She paused.

"Go on," I prompted.

"By the second round Carla fumed, 'What do I get grandmother?' I informed her that my entire fortune was in the eggs that her siblings found. I developed the plan to randomize the division of my estate. I told her that when she refused to hunt for eggs she gave up her inheritance."

"Wow," popped out of my mouth.

Blanche continued, "I'll never forget the slam of Carla's fist against the table. Her face hideous with hate as she screeched. "You old fool, this is ridiculous surely you're not going to leave me out?"

Blanche's words halted.

"What did you say to her?"

"I shook my head and said 'finders keepers.'"

"What a clever plan," I offered.

"Your psychological evaluation is Carla's attempt to control my estate. Contact my son if you think I'm feeble minded. He can take care of my business. I'll find his number here in my bag."

"Don't bother. I have no concerns about your mental health, which I will gladly put in my report."

Blanche stood, and delivered a hug over the walker grip. I followed her into the lobby.

"When will you have that report ready?" Carla demanded.

"Perhaps you would prefer it orally. I won't waste my time writing something you'll destroy. Blanche is fine, which I'll testify in court, should you oppose her will after her death."

"DAMN YOU," Carla's heels banged against the floor, as she tromped out the door.

"Marcy, please call a cab," Blanche quietly requested.

Von volunteered, "I'll do it."

Blanche offered an explanation to Von. "She's my granddaughter—disinherited her."

"You might consider giving her enough money to have the stick removed from her ass."

My mouth rounded in shock. "VON!"

"Oops, sorry Blanche, my mouth sometimes goes off before my brain is engaged."

Blanche's response was a trickle of a giggle that gradually erupted into a belly laugh. After a couple of minutes she gained control and looked at Von.

"Having that stick removed is a good idea, my boy."

CHAPTER TWENTY-TWO

HAYLEY AGAIN

Hayley, the woman so enraged at her first session that I thought she was going to explode, had my last appointment of the day. After an hour of EMDR therapy I handed her an appointment reminder for next week.

"What was that question from last time? The one I wouldn't answer?" Hayley asked.

"Your mother and Darren—did they have children?"

"Why?"

"A little girl around Darren is at risk."

"But Daisy is his biological daughter," Hayley reasoned.

"Usually doesn't matter to a pedophile. How old is Daisy?"

"She's around ten. Aunt Jade told me about her. I've never actually met her. You don't need to worry. Darren isn't living with her now."

"How do you know?"

"Jade said that Darren blew up the last time she called Mom. He told her Mom took off with Daisy. Darren also told her to quit nosing around his life."

"Does it surprise you that neither you nor your aunt heard this from your mother?"

"Not really. You know how our relationship ended. Mom and Aunt Jade were frequently at odds. Mom always needed a man to cling to. I'm sure she's found another one."

I slid a sheet of paper toward Hayley. "Write down their last known phone number and address."

Hayley hesitated, "Why?"

"I'll hire my private detective to find out if Darren is really alone. He may have lied to your aunt to keep her away."

Hayley accessed the information from her cell phone and jotted it down. "Call me if you find anything."

"I will."

Alone, I punched in Samuel's number. After describing my concerns, I said, "I'd like to come along for the ride."

His father-like tone conveyed doubt. "Not a good idea, Marcy. Never know about this stuff. Could be a boring night—or a dangerous one."

"Whichever, I want to watch you in action—see what I'm paying for."

"Lord help me. If you were anymore stubborn you'd turn into a mule."

"Aren't you the sweet talker?"

He laughed. "Meet me in front of Dinah's at 7 p.m."

"I'll be there," I promised.

"Unfortunately," he replied.

———◆———

I stepped into Samuel's truck at 6:55 p.m. The gun hanging from his waist stunned me. He must think it'll be a dangerous adventure not boring.

"Talked to the aunt," Samuel said. "She didn't know more than what you already told me. Darren does have a record. Served three years in prison—a convicted sex offender. Probably why he moved to the middle of nowhere."

The middle of nowhere was exactly where we ended up. A curving rock road, a one-way bridge, and complete darkness surrounded us as Samuel drove toward Darren's place.

"There's the fork where I go right. Based on Jade's directions, Darren's house is a mile up the road."

"What next?"

"I'll pull off near that fallen tree. I'm impressed that you had enough sense to wear black. You may be an adequate assistant after all."

I didn't admit my last-minute eureka moment that left a white sweatshirt thrown on my bedroom floor.

I followed close behind Samuel as he tromped toward Darren's house.

The growl came low and presaging, before breaking into a series of barks. Our canine greeter snarled, daring us to get closer.

"Stay back, mutt," Samuel warned.

Not an effective command. Mutt ran straight toward me, his yellow-fanged teeth ready to crunch my leg or whatever part he latched onto first.

The knife flew from Samuel's hand with pinpoint accuracy and stuck in the dog's neck. The dog's dead eyes transfixed on Samuel as if to ask, "What the hell happened?"

Samuel stepped forward and pulled out the knife. "Told you to back off, mutt."

I followed Samuel away from the road into the shadow of the underbrush. Soon the building, more like a shack than a house, came into view. Weather had grayed the wood and the result was the rotted demise of an unattached porch swing.

"Are we knocking on the door?" I whispered.

I barely heard his soft reply. "Maybe later. I'll look around first. You hide farther in the bushes." Samuel's feet quietly rustled toward the rear of the shack.

Alone in the shrubbery wasn't the assignment I wanted but Samuel had that bossy tone so I obeyed. I concentrated on night sounds, and the one light that peeked through the shack window. I thought I heard panting. Did mutt rise again to take me for his last meal? *Dead dogs aren't hungry.* I backed deeper into the underbrush. A tangle of branches caught my foot and threw me forward. I rolled into an indentation that cradled my body. I struggled up then bent down to explore the parameters of the sunken earth. It was my size—woman size—grave size.

A shot rang out and echoed through the woods. *Samuel!* Had Darren caught Samuel messing around his place?

Didn't really matter that Samuel kept the truck key, because I didn't have a clue as to how to find my way back to civilization. No way out for me.

"Marcy," Samuel hollered from the front porch. "Come on out. Darren's dead."

Worry sprang into my head as I ran. *Dead?* Checking a place out was a distant activity from killing a man.

His words blurted as I reached the porch steps. "Caught him raping her. I did what had to be done."

He offered no description of self-defense.

"Come talk to the child."

I raced into the shack. A child lay naked on an old mattress. "Daisy?" An animalistic fear contorted her features.

"Mommy?" she whimpered, as Samuel dragged the man's dead body away from her.

"We'll take you someplace safe." I tried to touch her, but she rolled away.

"Mommy?" she cried, again. Her small blue eyes, underscored by black circles, looked toward the door.

"I know your sister, Hayley. Did your mommy tell you about her?"

Daisy's words were soft, but matter-of-fact. "Daddy said he killed her 'cause she didn't mind him and he'd do the same to me."

"Hayley is fine. I'll take you to her," I promised.

"Daddy dead?"

"Yes, he was a bad man."

"Okay," she said.

I looked around for a comforting toy for our trip into town. A couple of ragged shirts and a pair of torn jeans were all I found. No toys in that shack for a child.

Darkness gloomed around us as I followed Samuel. He carried Daisy toward the truck.

A blood-curdling scream pierced my ears when I attempted to click her seatbelt. I gave up and cuddled her on my lap. After a few miles, a flickering gas station sign signaled our return to humanity.

The flashing welcome sign made shadows across Samuel's wrinkled face as he stood in the open air, phoning local law enforcement.

Less than ten minutes later an ambulance arrived followed by a patrol car.

"Samuel, I'm going with Daisy."

He acknowledged me with a wave then returned to the sheriff's questions.

The ambulance's siren announced our arrival, and hospital staff ran out the emergency room door.

"Do we need a rape kit?" The nurse asked as she wheeled Daisy down the hall.

"Yes, child has likely been assaulted numerous times."

"We'll take her directly to the sexual assault examination room," the nurse said.

With Daisy in safe hands, I called Hayley.

"Hayley, it's Marcy. Daisy's being admitted to River's Bend Hospital. A next of kin needs to fill out the paperwork."

A short silence, then she asked, "Where are Mom and Darren?"

"Your mom wasn't there. Darren is dead, caught in the act of raping Daisy."

"Where's the hospital?"

"I'll hand the phone to an ambulance attendant to give you directions."

Hayley's words rushed against each other. "Okay, I'll be there soon."

No use telling Hayley my assumption about her mother. The local sheriff could handle that.

A few minutes later Samuel, and the sheriff, entered the waiting room.

"Miss Simon?" The haggard, gun-toting man motioned me to a private room. "You stay here, Samuel."

An overhead light flickered in the small room. The sheriff motioned toward a card table and a wood chair. I sat on the hard surface.

He remained standing. "My men are at the shooting site. Tell me what happened."

"You need to know something. I tripped and fell into a cradle of sunken earth about fifteen yards out and east of the house. When we didn't find Daisy's mom I feared the worst. Afraid she was buried in the woods."

He flattened his palms on the table and leaned toward me.

"That's quite an imagination you have."

"I know, sorry. Daisy's sister told me her mother left Darren, but Daisy still lived with the monster. So what happened to Daisy's mom?"

"I'll check out your story."

"Thank you."

"Tell me how Darren ended up dead?"

I described the events. Glad that I wasn't a witness to the actual shooting. I found it impossible to believe that Samuel killed Darren in self-defense. Considering he had the element of surprise and Darren was in the process of raping a child.

I clearly stated the position of Darren's naked body that Samuel pulled off Daisy. Sheriff's complexion turned gray as I described the blood-mixed semen on the child's leg.

"I'm going to the site. If you think of anything else call me."

"Yes, sir."

"Jot down your contact information."

I steadied my hand in an attempt to make the numerals legible.

He snatched the paper, and headed out the door.

"Marcy Simon?" the doctor questioned.

"Yes."

"Daisy's family here?"

"Not yet. Can I help?"

"Please come back. Can't stop Daisy's crying."

I sat beside Daisy. Her sobs lessened to intermediate moans. "I'm sorry Daisy I know this hurts, but they need to examine you, and give medicine to make you feel better. Your daddy will never hurt you again. I promise."

An hour later hurried footsteps sounded outside our curtained space. Hayley slowed as she walked toward Daisy. She reached a pink teddy bear toward her. Daisy scrunched the comfort toy to her chest. Her moans stopped.

"Daisy, I'm your sister. Hayley's my name." Hayley petted Daisy's head. "Do you like the bear?"

Daisy kissed the bear's snout.

The doctor looked at me. "One of you can accompany Daisy to the x-ray room."

"Her sister is here," I responded.

I touched Daisy's face, then squeezed Hayley's arm. "I'll be in touch. Call if you need anything. She's going to require therapy to overcome what she's been through, but no one knows that better than you."

"We can do it with your help, Marcy."

"I know you can."

I returned to the waiting room. Samuel was talking to a tall, thin, redheaded man, who turned out to be Hayley's husband.

"How they doing?" Samuel asked.

"Okay."

"Did she like the bear?" The redhead questioned.

"Loved it, hugged it tight."

"Bear was my idea. Hayley said we didn't have time, but it only took an extra five minutes."

"A good use of time," I acknowledged.

"I always wanted kids. Who would've thought we'd start with a ten-year-old?"

What Hayley told me about her husband being a good guy seemed true. Hopefully, he was the daddy that Daisy needed to help her heal.

"Can we head out now, Samuel? Or must we hang around for the sheriff?"

"He knows where to find me."

Outside the door, Samuel pulled me to a stop.

"Sheriff said it was a grave, and likely the remains inside are Daisy's mom."

"Not always good to be right. Sometimes wrong is best."

"True enough," Samuel confirmed. "Let's get out of here. Long day."

CHAPTER TWENTY-THREE

PEGGY AGAIN

Saturday morning came at rocket speed. I checked messages three times while I ate cereal. Showered and then ran to the phone hoping I'd heard from Samuel. I kept it beside me as I dressed. My worried state continued as I drove to the shelter. No new information so no idea what to tell Peggy about her stalker husband. Why didn't I think to ask Samuel last night? I knew the answer—too much drama.

As soon as I arrived at my office my nervous fingers pushed in his number for the fifth or sixth time. The machine peeped a summons to leave a message. "Samuel, it's Marcy. I'm at the shelter. Peggy is due here in thirty minutes. I need your information."

The closed phone rested in my hand. Perhaps I could caress it into playing its tune, but no—nothing. Ten minutes later I paced. Peggy probably wouldn't show anyway—not the reliable sort.

I startled when a firm knock sounded. A white bushy head poked in the door opening.

The chair scraped as Samuel pulled it forward then sat. "Sorry, about the wait Marcy. Got my final confirmation on Peggy's husband this morning."

"Confirmation?"

"Peggy's husband is in prison, where he has resided for the last three years."

"So who's following her?"

"No one that I saw. Mostly spends her time picking fights, cussing, and threatening. I was outside her place one night when the cops showed up. Peggy claimed her ex threw a rock through the back window. I saw her throw it. I reported what I saw to a cop. He said she was bleeding. She must've cut herself."

"Unbelievable," I retorted.

Samuel stood. "What do you think is wrong with her?"

"Sounds like hysterical personality disorder but she needs observed and tested to confirm."

"What's hysterical personality disorder?" Samuel asked

"She's grandiose, narcissistic, and attention seeking."

Samuel shook his head. "I don't know about all those fancy words, just seems like a crazy liar."

"Got a bill?" I asked.

"Yep," He pulled a yellow form out of his pocket.

I scribbled out a check as I spoke. "One more thing. Will you deliver a confidential package to a precinct outside this area?"

"Why not local?"

"Don't want Zane in my business. It's probably nothing, but it's important to know if the DNA on these jockeys matches the DNA found at the prostitute murder site." I handed him the bag. "Don't divulge where you got them. If there's a match I'll deal with the repercussions when they erupt."

"I'll deliver the bag right now to a cop buddy. Going out of town. That sheriff called me in to answer more questions about Darren's death."

"Thanks."

"Anytime," Samuel offered a firm handshake then exited.

Samuel, a male who didn't ask probing questions—my favorite kind of man.

A few minutes later, after I decided she was a no show, Peggy's bandaged arm swung open my door.

"You ready for me?"

"I see you're hurt."

"That deranged fool broke the kitchen window, then stabbed me with the glass. I tell you I'll be dead soon."

"Why didn't he kill you?"

"Said he would next time. Wanted to wait, and give himself a nice birthday present next month."

"Peggy, we'll find you someplace safe," I soothed.

"Why didn't you do that before he broke my window and cut me?" Spit sprinkled out with each word.

"I was worried, so I had a detective follow you. He saw you break the window."

Her fist pounded my desk. "You calling me a liar?"

"You're ill, Peggy. Tom hasn't been following you. He's in prison. Remember?"

She slouched in the chair, eyes focused on the ceiling light. "Don't recollect him going."

"He's in Mississippi, perhaps no one told you. Still you've been seeing and accusing him. Maybe hallucinations. We've got to get you help. I phoned the Behavioral Health Unit at the hospital. You'll go inpatient for observation and tests."

"Ain't going to no loony bin."

"You're ill, Peggy. If I understand correctly you don't have family to help."

"Maybe I was lying about my old man." She grinned. "Maybe I didn't see him at all."

"Perhaps deviousness is more mentally unstable than actually believing the stalking was real."

There was a firm tap and I opened the door to a tall, thin man dressed in scrubs. An older male, built like a pro wrestler, stood behind thin guy. "Ready, Ms. Simon?" he asked.

"These two men will drive you to the hospital."

"Sons-of-bitches ain't taking me nowhere." Peggy grabbed a book, and flung it toward them.

Thin guy slapped it to the floor, and moved toward her.

"Wait," I directed. "Listen, Peggy, you either go with these guys or go to jail. You've made false accusations and destroyed property. I'm sure they can find plenty of other charges. Your choice: jail bunk or a soft bed, good meals and people to help you sort out your problems. Your choice."

The flamboyant woman faded.

"I'll go."

"A good choice, Peggy. I wish you well."

———— ◆ ————

I tracked Maybelle down in the kitchen.

"Girl, you look like you're in need of chicken and dumplings."

"That may cure all my problems," I laughed.

"Tough morning?" Maybelle spooned my lunch into a bowl.

"The worst."

She wrapped soft arms around me. "Here's a hug."

"That makes me feel better."

She reached the bowl toward me. "These here dumplings will finish the job."

My bowl half empty I heard familiar voices in the lobby: Zane and Sonya.

I sprang from the stool. "Got to go!"

"You're not finished little gal. You act like your ass is on fire."

"I hear the voice of doom," I whispered.

"Zane?"

"That's him—my nosey nemesis."

Footsteps sounded outside the door. I ducked into the pantry.

"Maybelle, where's Marcy?"

She stirred the pot. "Here earlier."

Through the crack in the door I saw Zane touch the side of my chicken bowl.

"Bowl is still hot, Maybelle."

"Maybe that's my bowl Mr. Investigator. You going to take a DNA sample?" she huffed.

"Not this time. Tell her I'm sorry for being an asshole the other night."

"I'd be mighty pleased to deliver the apology. I'm thinking you're sweet on that little gal."

"Don't tell her that, she'd probably try to get away with more shit."

"Oh, I won't tell. You run on now I got a kitchen to clean."

"Sure thing," he obliged.

I peeked out the door. My emotions mixed, got an apology, and an insult to cancel it out.

"You heard all that Marcy?"

"I did, thanks for covering."

"Anytime."

"Heading home. See you next Saturday."

Her arms circled me. For just a second I pretended it was Zane holding me, but Maybelle's too fluffy for that fantasy to last.

CHAPTER TWENTY-FOUR

PROSTITUTE KILLER

"Hello Dinah." I spoke into my cell phone as Von placed client files on my office desk.

"Zane and a couple of detectives were in the diner looking for Samuel. Thought you might know what's up, and where he is."

"He had business out of town this morning but should be back soon."

"Glad to know he's okay. Got people to feed. Bye."

I pressed my chest to keep my heart from jumping out. This can only mean one thing—the DNA on the jockeys matched criminal activity somewhere. I'll be raked over the coals for information. My brain refused to formulate an escape plan.

"Von!"

He bowed, "Yes, my majesty."

"Please sit."

"What's up, Marcy? You're a new shade of pale."

"They'll come for me."

"Aliens? Naked dancing men—whoops that's my fantasy."

My smile snuck out in spite of anxiety. "My fantasy, too, but not today."

His eyes squinted, "Tell me."

"Detectives were looking for Samuel at the diner this morning."

"Is it because he shot Hayley's stepdad?"

"No, that's why Samuel is out of town today. That sheriff called him in for more questioning."

Von's mouth gaped. "Oh, oh that means…"

"Means I'm doomed. All because of Celeste and her stupid sex experiment."

"Those three aren't real clients. You're not breaching confidentiality if you talk to the police."

"Doesn't look good for a psychologist to get involved in manipulating men's lives. I'm road kill."

Von scratched his head. "What are you going to tell the police?"

My cell phone vibrated against the wood desk. I spied the name on the caller ID and snatched the phone.

"Marcy, it's Samuel. City cops are giving me the hard line. Say they're going to lock me up if I don't divulge who gave me the dirty undies."

"Are you back in town?"

"Yes. I'm on my way to the police station right now. Ordered me to arrive within the hour, or they'd send a patrol car."

My labored breathing filled a pause. "I don't know what to do, Samuel."

"Don't do anything. I never rat on clients. Even if they jail me my mouth stays clamped."

"It's more than protecting me. If Monty Matthews is the killer, more women will die if I don't tell the truth."

"Are you sure, Marcy? You don't have to get involved."

"Tell them I'm on my way. Where to?"

"Back at the local station," Samuel said before hanging up.

Von stood, "Sounds like you made a decision."

"Only one choice."

"Thought you'd get there."

"Then why didn't you show me the light?" I rubbed the back of my neck.

"The repercussions may change your life."

"So if I'm going to screw up my life, it's my decision alone."

"Exactly!"

———◆———

A female officer escorted me into a stark room. Samuel sat on one side of a table in a straight wood chair. Two detectives, plus Zane, sat on the other side in cushioned swivel chairs. Zane's hand waved me to the wood chair next to Samuel. Perhaps the lack of seat cushions was an advanced interrogation method. People may spill their guts if their butts hurt.

"Samuel, I'll have an officer take you to a holding room while we talk to Ms. Simon." The nasty Zane attitude wasn't present. His eyes looked pleadingly into mine. Took a minute, but I got it. If I divulged Zane had prior knowledge of the underwear, he'd look bad to his cohorts, not to mention his boss.

"First, Samuel only delivered the jockeys, he had no other role. He should be released."

The pug-nosed detective's eyes squinted. "I'm thinking we'll detain him for a spell."

My chair squealed as I pushed back. "I might as well go because you're not going to believe a word I say."

"I believe you," the bald-headed detective stated. "You're dismissed, Samuel."

Samuel nodded toward me. I touched his arm, "I'm okay."

"Your buddy is free," Pug said. "It's time for your story. Better be true or I'll hunt Samuel down and lock him up."

Disgust tightened Baldy's features. His unspoken words pierced into Pug's face.

"Marcy, right?"

"Yes, Marcy Simon."

"Who do these shorts belong to, Marcy?" He pointed to a plastic bag in the middle of the table.

"What did the man do?" I asked.

"That's not your business." Pug again.

"Matched DNA on a murder victim's bed." Zane answered.

Zane's answer to my question another indication he was playing nice. He wanted my mouth shut regarding his previous case knowledge.

Zane continued, "It's very important that we find this guy.

We appreciate your help."

Pug looked like he was going to barf in his coffee.

Baldy joined in with Zane's calm "help us" approach. "We'll keep you out of this as much as the legal system allows. We just need information."

Pug's eyes rolled.

"That guy," I pointed at Pug, "Makes me nervous rolling his eyes and fisting the air. Tell him to leave or I'm not talking."

"Go," Baldy directed. "You're making the witness squeamish."

The swivel chair hit the floor, as Pug banged from the room. Pug's exclusion was a small victory—likely my only one that day.

"Two pairs of eyes stared at me. Waiting for me to spill my guts, so I did. "I have a friend who's a prostitute."

"What's her name?" Baldy's pen ready to write.

I ignored the question. "A customer of hers became violent when she wouldn't give him head. He went for her throat. The underwear is his."

Baldy interrupted, "She gave them to you?"

"I asked Samuel to turn them in to his cop friend. Unlikely this man's a killer, but for some reason the murders stuck in my head after I witnessed his violent reaction."

Damn, I screwed up.

Baldy's head cocked sideways. "You watched the john and prostitute have sex?"

"His wife wanted his faithfulness tested—he failed."

Agitation rippled through Baldy's words. "You're leaving a lot out of this story."

"Yes, I must protect my client."

"And yourself?"

"Yes," I acknowledged. "Will you promise to keep my name out of this mess if I talk?"

Baldy sounded a bit worn. "Yes, to the best of my ability. Who's the man?"

"Name is Monty Matthews. By all accounts a model citizen, wealthy, and hardworking. Not a man who looks like a killer."

Zane's silence lifted. "Did you learn anything else about Matthews from your client?"

"Monty is violent with her also, and…"

Zane's voice now earnest. "And what, Marcy?"

"His wife, Leeza, said that Monty has a stash of panties in his tool box in the garage—some bloody."

The furrows in Baldy's face flattened. "Shit, we may actually catch this guy."

Zane agreed with a nod.

Baldy barked orders. "Zane, call the captain. We'll get a search warrant from a district judge. Shouldn't take more than a couple of hours. If the DNA on the panties matches the victims we'll have the murders solved tonight. Anything else we should know, Ms. Simon?"

"That's all."

"You can go," Baldy directed.

I walked out the door as the captain's rapid footsteps pushed toward me—Pug trailed behind. A glaring side-glance was my only goodbye.

I felt unsure and apprehensive as I drove slowly home. No doubt Matthews was a bad man who needed to be stopped. Leeza, my unofficial client, would get caught in a sex and murder drama with her two young children. I knew the emotional impact on children of having a parent handcuffed and carted off in a police cruiser. Whether their father proved to be guilty or not the children would face a traumatic situation. *What have I done?*

Parked in my apartment space. I brought up Leeza's number.

"Leeza, it's Marcy Simon. Get your children out of the house right now."

"Why? What's going on?" Her voice went from calm to frantic in seconds.

"I can't tell you. Just take your children to a hotel and don't ask questions."

Her voice in panic mode, "What have you done?"

"Told the truth. I'm calling to protect your children. If you want them safe take them away from your house. Don't tell Monty about this—just go."

My shaking hand pushed the off button. The phone call, and perhaps my career, terminated.

———— ♦ ————

The pounding started a little after midnight. I opened the door to three faces with different degrees of rage etched into their brows and lips. Von spent the night with a "friend," so I faced the firing squad alone in a pink nightgown with a white robe pulled tightly around my body. The trio didn't sit but stood in a semicircle in front of me.

"There was nothing." Pug raved. Baldy didn't try to suppress him.

The captain stood stiff, his hands fisted in and out as if eager to get my neck in his grasp. "The place was clean. The family gone."

"You made fools out of us." Pug muttered through a clenched jaw.

Baldy's accusatory stare sunk into my eyes. "What did you do, Simon?"

"It would've harmed the children—emotionally—to be there. I phoned Leeza, and told her to spend the night at a hotel."

The captain's hands now hung clenched in the air. "You cued the couple to get rid of the evidence. Even if we manage to eventually tag him for one murder the other two will go unprosecuted, because there's no connection to Matthews."

"By the way," the captain's stone face inches from mine, "I interviewed Matthews. So cool, and righteous sitting in his big leather desk chair he left a chill in the air. He admitted sleeping with the prostitute, said he's a little sexually perverted, but swore he's no killer. Even shed a few tears at the prospect of his wife and friends finding out about his prostitution habit."

I backed away. "You believed him?"

He stepped back into my personal space. "You left me with no other choice."

"Call the wife," captain ordered. "We want to hear the conversation."

I punched in her number and put the phone on speaker.

Her voice screeched. "What do you want now? Why are you ruining my life?"

"I protected your children from a police search. You're

obviously more interested in covering for Monty."

"He's all I got—my home, my money, my children's expensive private school depend on him."

"If he's a killer?"

"He's a pervert, which doesn't make him a murderer."

"You told me about the bloody panties."

Her words grounded into my head. "I lied, wanted to shock you."

I yelled into the phone. "His semen matched the DNA at a murder scene."

"That's not too surprising since he's a sex addict. Probably lots of men's semen in a whore's bed. One of many, I'm sure. Stay away from my family, or I'll ruin you personally and professionally." The line went dead.

"She's right," the captain said, "six other DNA samples from the same bed, and none of them may be the killer. Murderer may not even have had sex with the victim. The panties were our only hope to pair Monty with the women, now the wife claims they never existed."

Baldy's words stabbed at my conscience. "He'll continue killing. Thanks to you, Simon."

I looked at the captain, "I'm sorry."

"Pug yipped, "She should be arrested for interfering with our case."

"I'm not charging you with obstruction of justice, because I gave my word I'd keep your report anonymous." The captain gave a final sneer, then waved his men out the door.

The final slam resonated in my head as I walked toward my bed. I laid flat on my back, my eyes wide open, and my brain in turmoil. I asked myself why I didn't weigh the outcome more carefully. Two traumatized children or more dead women. Baldy was correct. The murderer would continue killing because of me.

CHAPTER TWENTY-FIVE

A KILLER'S NEW WOMAN

Up and down, down and up, then circling the chair. Denise stopped and grasped her ponytail. The clothes she wore hung loosely. The pants held up by boney hips and the crop-top exposed meatless ribs.

Denise's fingers intertwined in her oily brown hair as she spoke. "Man, I got to get out of here, Ms. Simon."

"Out of the Women's Shelter?"

"Out of this town. Bethel's going to kill me."

My body tightened. An unusual name—was she talking about Sidney's ex?

"How long have you been with Bethel?"

"Together five or six months. Had a job, not bad looking so I screwed him. One thing led to another and we shacked up."

"Why is he angry?"

"Pissed when I used drugs a little. He went ballistic because money was missing from his wallet. He slapped me around. I told him I was leaving his sorry, mean ass."

"How did he respond?"

"He belly punched me. He said I wasn't going anywhere until I found his two hundred bucks. If I didn't take it one of my druggie friends did. If not them than my sleazy family swiped it. Told me I better figure it out or I'd be skinned."

"What next?"

"Told him his family name should be Shit since that described everyone of his relatives. One of them took his money cause me and mine didn't."

Denise touched her swollen left eye. It looked like a bulb with a thin opening down the middle.

"Said his hard-earned money wasn't going for drugs. Yelled like a lunatic that his cash better return by seven tonight or somebody would have to scrape my remains off the sidewalk."

"Do you think he's that violent?"

"Told him he wasn't man enough to kill me. Talked a good game, but I'd seen him back off men plenty of times. Damn, so mad his ears turned red, and sweat dripped from his chin. He looked straight at me with those beady eyes and yelled, 'I killed one bitch and I don't mind doing a second. Freaked me out."

My heart drummed. "How did you get away?"

"I started thinking I better play it cool or end up on a slab. I said, I'd check around to see if anyone I knew was tossing bills around. No way am I going back to his place, but it won't take long for him to find me. He's got spies everywhere." Denise took a breath.

My chest tightened, "Who was the woman he killed?"

"Must've meant that Sidney chick, 'cause she died in his house."

I leaned forward, "Did he name her?"

"He's mean not stupid."

"Denise, you can stay at the shelter for thirty days. That'll keep you under his radar. We'll find you a place to relocate."

"Don't want to leave my friends and family."

"Staying in this town is a death sentence. We know he killed one woman. There's no doubt he'd do the same to you."

A look of doom and gloom surfaced. "Isn't fair that I have to give up my life."

"I know… there may be an alternative."

Her eyes widened, "I'll take it!"

"Hold up a second. You haven't heard what it is."

She finally sunk into the chair and stayed. "Anything is better than starting over."

"If Bethel is jailed for Sidney's murder you'd be safe."

"Go on."

"You'd tell the police what you told me. Probably have to testify in court."

"If he ever gets out I'd be dead meat."

"Another man received a life sentence for Sidney's murder. You'd save yourself and him."

Denise jumped up, "Guy's rotting in prison?"

"Sid's brother came to help her leave Bethel. Bethel set him up and yes, he's been in prison for at least five years."

"Damn that sucks, if he didn't do anything."

"Would you be willing to testify to stay in your home town and save a stranger?"

Her hand pulled at her ponytail. "Bethel is liable to kill me."

"It's a possibility."

Denise's face toughened, "That bastard isn't forcing me away from my family. Let's bring him down."

"Let's," I said. "I'll call a policeman to take your statement." I found the number and pecked it into my phone.

"Zane, it's Marcy. Have a woman at the shelter who reports that Bethel admitted to killing a woman."

"Say who he murdered?"

"No, but Sid's the only dead body ever picked up at his house, as far as I know."

"I'll be right there."

———— ◆ ————

Zane looked official when he came in my door, also quite handsome. Baldy sauntered in behind him.

Denise repeated her story for the pair.

Zane's dark eyes delved into her blue ones. "Did he describe the actual murder?"

"Showed me how he plunged the knife into her chest, then twisted. The blood gushed out like a fountain. He laughed when he told me."

"Anything else?" Baldy asked.

Denise's hyper movement halted. "Can't think of anything. Can I go now? No sleep last night."

"Out of curiosity," Zane said, "did you take Bethel's cash?"

"What if I did?"

"Nothing. No theft reported."

A flirty grin aimed at Baldy. "I got me a couple of bad habits to finance."

Baldy crowed out the words, "I get it!"

"Go upstairs," I directed Denise. "Supper at 5:30. You have time to shower and nap. Extra clothes in the hall closet."

"I'm gone," Denise called as she exited.

"Later," Zane responded.

"Is it enough?" I asked the pair.

"Maybe," Zane answered.

Baldy looked at Zane. "But Bethel didn't say who he killed."

"Denise described the stabbing that would've resulted in the wound found in Sidney's body." Zane paused and turned at the door. "We'll review all case information, maybe find a loophole that Bethel can fall into. We'll report to the captain. I'll give you a heads up, Marcy, if something moves."

"Thanks," I said.

The men gone I pulled an old newspaper out of the bottom desk drawer. Guilt bubbled in my head as I looked at Sid's photo. *Was I about to get Denise killed, too?*

CHAPTER TWENTY-SIX

PRISON

I'd never visited prison—quite the new way to spend Sunday afternoon. A fence so high I practically dislocated my neck to view the electric wire topper. Everything seemed gray. Even the red bricks were marred with a smoky gray tinge. Wall paint and tiles continued the gray color scheme inside.

An official had run me through their procedures. May be harder to obtain admittance to a prison than escape. Eventually, he escorted me out of his cubby, and pointed toward the check-in counter.

Personal chatter on her cell phone kept the clerk occupied for seven minutes while I waited.

Patience gone, I slammed my purse on the counter. "Excuse me. Do you work here? Where's the visiting area?"

Fiery-eyed, she used her middle finger to point out a guard stationed down the hall.

I fluttered my middle finger in the air, "Thanks."

Every guard I passed looked the same—hollow eyed with frozen pupils. I wondered if there was a masochist among them who enjoyed the job of herding the barbarians of society. I'd be afraid every minute of every shift. Always waiting for a monster to grab my throat, and twist the life out. The criminal faces that I passed shot their evil glances through me into nothingness. Shivers ran up my arms.

I trailed behind a guard to the visiting area. I attempted friendliness, but he didn't respond. His eyes flittered back and forth to the right, to the left and back behind. Not unlike an animal ready to defend himself. He stopped abruptly and pointed to a man on the other side of a barrier.

What am I doing here? This was no helpless boy. His shaved pinhead topped a massive muscular frame. He looked like a killer. My chest ached from tension or maybe terror is a better descriptive word.

I don't ever have to come back—one conversation, then leave. My hands squeezed my knees as I looked into his face.

Jerry growled, "Who are you?"

"Marcy Simon. I knew your sister."

"What do you want?"

"I need to know if you're worth saving. Did you kill Sidney?"

"That's why I'm caged. They decided I murdered the only person on earth I cared about or cared about me."

"Did you?"

His words shot out, "NO, for the millionth time, NO."

"I didn't think so, just wanted to hear it from you."

"You got some magic truth serum?"

"I think I read people pretty well."

He squeezed his nostrils then swiped the snot across his shirt shoulder.

"Sidney called me that day—said you were helping her move."

"That was the plan. Bethel must've snuck in and killed her when I took a truckload to my house. When I got back I found her in the bathtub. Guess he didn't want blood on his carpet."

"The newspaper said Bethel had an alibi," I offered.

"He owns a garage. His fellow turds covered for him." The venom returned, "I been here five years. Why you showing up now?"

"The evidence indicated your guilt." *A feeble excuse for letting a man rot in prison for five years.*

"But here you sit."

"Can't get your sister out of my mind. I saw the anger in Bethel's face once. If he'd grown horns—he could've been the devil himself."

"Your fantasy isn't proving me innocent."

"There's new evidence. A person reported that Bethel admitted to killing a woman. Your case may be reopened. I can't promise you anything, but don't give up. You have a reputation for being a troublemaker. It's time to stop acting like a criminal. Hard to convince people you should be free when there's a boulder-sized chip on your shoulder." *Brave words or stupid, when delivered to a criminal, but there's a screen between us and an armed guard six feet away.*

He scowled, "How do you know?"

"Talked to your lawyer. He didn't want to work any new case of yours because you're apparently a foul-mouthed, mean bastard." I watched Jerry's reaction, waiting for him to blow. He didn't.

He rubbed his chin. "Yep, got good reason."

"I can't argue that, but this is your last chance. Can you act civilized or do I need to forget you?"

The attitude drained from his face. "I can do it."

"Okay, I hired a new lawyer, J.R. Terrance. He'll be here Monday morning. Play nice." I grinned.

"Why are you doing this for me?"

"For your sister—I owe her."

CHAPTER TWENTY-SEVEN

SEX HATER—LYDIA

Monday through Friday morning came and went without fanfare. Only two clients stood between the weekend and me. Von was having a therapy session with Damon. I listened intently for my first afternoon client.

Her door knock was barely discernible. "Come in," I called.

The woman's nose twitched like a bunny sniffing for food. "I'm so sorry. Must be early. I'll wait in the lobby."

"You're fine. Lydia?"

"Yes," she whimpered.

"Glad you made it. Wasn't sure you'd come when we spoke on the phone."

She sat slumped at the chair's edge. "I almost backed out. Wasted money to see a psychologist for an unsolvable problem."

"Would you like a beverage?"

"Don't bother," she whined.

"It isn't a problem. Coffee?"

"Okay," she said.

"Sugar and cream?"

"Too much trouble," Lydia signed. "Black is fine."

Lydia reminded me of that depressed donkey on *Winnie*

the Pooh cartoons. "Would you like cream and sugar?" *Maybe I need to call in a consulting physician to arrange a backbone replacement.*

"Well... I..."

"Tell me what you want."

"Cream and sugar, I guess."

"One pack or two?"

"Doesn't matter."

I should've taken pain pills before Lydia arrived. My head felt like it may explode.

I walked toward the coffeemaker and poured her a cup. "Lydia, one pack or two?"

"Two, thank you."

"You're welcome." I handed her the cup. She sipped gently before her eyes rounded as she caught me watching her. As if a child caught in mischief.

"Lydia, why are you here?"

"I'm a fool."

"You aren't allowed to call yourself names in my office."

A sheepish, "Sorry."

"Tell me your problem."

"I hate my husband," her tone low.

"When did you get married?"

"Ceremony two weeks ago." Her front teeth bit into her bottom lip. A bubble of blood broke through. "Stupid, stupid to give up this soon."

"Do you want your marriage saved?"

"I don't know."

According to the intake form, she was thirty-five and recently married to a man named Larry. No facial character lines, little eye movement, and most of her comments were directed toward the floor. Dressed in a shapeless, flowered housedress.

"When did you decide that Larry wasn't the man for you?"

"On our honeymoon. We went to Mexico."

I nodded.

Lydia pressed a tissue against her forehead. "We'd only known each other two weeks. He was nice and patient. Didn't try any nasty stuff. Told me he loved me at first sight, and didn't want to lose me. I married him. In my thirties, no past boyfriends, I saw him as the opportunity to have a life partner."

"Then?"

Her face rested in her hands. "I can't talk about this."

"Sex?"

Lydia's body swayed side-to-side.

I asked her to rise while I turned the indigo chair toward the door. My hand waved her to sit back down. "You'll be more comfortable without me in front of you."

She obeyed—of course.

I leaned against my desk, directly behind her. "Describe your problem in one sentence?"

She didn't hesitate or stutter, "I hate sex."

"Is it painful?"

"Wish it was, then I'd have an excuse."

"What do you hate about intercourse?"

Her head rocked forward. "I despise semen. It's slivery, mushy, gross."

"Were you sexually abused?"

"No."

"Generally there's a cause for an aversion. Something in your history that grew the phobia."

A nervous laugh escaped. "Do you think sperm traumatized me?"

She has a sense of humor—unexpected.

I continued, "Not exactly, but maybe there's something related."

"I know men like that nasty stuff." Lydia pulled at her dress hem as if some guy might try to get a peek. "Mom said husbands expected sex, craved it, went nuts over it. Now that I'm a wife I'd have to shut up and put up. I was determined to do my wifely duty."

I broke into her story. "Determination is a good trait."

"Our first night I wore a red sexy nightgown. He rubbed my back, and gently touched—down there."

"Did it feel good?"

"It did, I'm embarrassed to say. I massaged his back and rubbed his man part. When I let loose of it he kissed me. I gagged for a second when his tongue probed my mouth. He rolled me over. He humped and humped, something shot into my body. I felt it running down my leg. A gross wet spot touched my back as I rolled off the bed. I ran to the bathroom.

The shower water steamed around me as I scrubbed off the goop."

"Did he say anything to you?"

"He called from outside the locked door. 'Are you okay, Lydia? Did I hurt you?'

I told him to go away and I scrubbed some more."

"How long did you shower?"

"Probably an hour. When I came back in the bedroom he stayed on the far side of the bed facing the wall. Too mad or sad to talk, because I'd hurt his feelings. I couldn't help it."

"You felt bad because of his reaction?"

She stood and faced me. "I did and do. Something about Larry touched my heart, but I can't stand intimacy. I need a divorce, don't I?"

"No."

"He deserved better."

"He chose you. You're who he wanted."

"But I'm not a real wife."

"You can be." I quietly assured her.

Her face puckered. "No, I can't. It's too gross."

"It's all about figuring out what's going on inside your head. My theory is that you don't hate sex. You despise something that you connect with sex. Define semen for me."

Disgust twisted her face, "Yucky."

"Define it like a word in the dictionary," I instructed.

"A white, slimy substance that's forced into me."

"Does that relate to anything in your history?"

"I've never been raped, if that's what you mean."

"Certainly that's one possibility, but it doesn't apply to you. Think about where this hate originated."

"I have no idea."

"Any white food, beverages, creams, or medicines?"

Lydia's eyes lit up. "When my stomach ached, Mom gave me a spoonful of a white medicine. I'd spit it out, then she'd force the spoon to the back of my mouth. I'd gag then sometimes throw up. By this time she was so mad she'd call Dad to hold me down while she crammed the stuff down my throat. Eventually I quit telling Mom if my belly hurt. Do you think that's what caused me to hate man juice?"

"I know it sounds unrelated, but our brains have a way of

redefining bad experiences. Do you like the feeling of lotion on your skin?"

"Yes."

"Close your eyes and calm yourself. Think of warm, thick lotion. Rub it on your face. Lotion feels good, warm, soft. Relate the lotion to the semen, it feels soft and warm. Now open your eyes."

"What was that for?" Lydia's words stammered.

"It's called guided visualization. We'll use visualization to work on your problem during our next sessions. You'll learn to mentally re-associate your sensations with semen to a substance you like, even enjoy. For whatever the reason, you associate sex with negative, out-of-control feelings. Perhaps it stems from parents forcing the nasty tasting medicine down your throat. Likely we'll never know why."

Lydia twisted her hands together. "Does this mean I'm mentally ill?"

"I define your problem as a low-level phobia, not a mental disorder."

"You think I'll be okay?"

"I do. Your first assignment is to tell your husband about this issue even though it embarrasses you. Tell him you're working on it and need his help. Assure him he's done nothing wrong."

A gentle giggle then Lydia spoke, "He needs to know I don't like to screw, because I'm a bit screwed up?"

I smiled. "Just a little, but I'm optimistic you'll be able to work this out."

She stood, her eyes focused on mine. "Same time next week?"

"I'll be here."

"Me too," Lydia sang out.

A smile stayed on my lips after she exited. *Once in a while I do good.*

CHAPTER TWENTY-EIGHT

SCREW THE WITCH

Nausea swayed my stomach as she walked into my office. The witch arrived like a loaded cement truck, and parked her ass in the chair across from my desk. Her mouth drooped at both ends.

"Gretta," the word sprang out.

"Yep, it's me scraping the barrel bottom."

Not sure if she meant I was the bottom or that she'd bottomed out emotionally. Actually, I do know she meant me. I wore my professional persona anyway. I squeezed my hands together, so I wouldn't strangle her and proceeded.

"Gretta, why are you here?"

She swiveled and surveyed my office. "Guess things turned out all right for you—fancy office and expensive clothes. Considering you tried to sex your way into keeping a job, can't say you deserved success."

"Surely you're not paying for this session to discuss my past. Some of which I do regret, but the bottom line is it's none of your business."

Gretta's nostrils flared. "The head doctor is defensive. Didn't think counselors were supposed to be hateful to patients."

"I'm not here to comfort. I help people develop plans to

solve their own problems. Start telling me yours or leave. I don't have time to waste."

The left side of her lip curled. "Summed up, I married a wimpy man. It's a wonder George can stand considering his jelly backbone. Tells everybody 'yes.' He'll help his mom every Saturday. Assist some guy at work on Sundays. Seldom free to work at my house. He finally did the Friday night dishes on Sunday morning. His lame excuse being he didn't get the dishes washed because his mom wasn't feeling well. Claimed he didn't want to leave her alone. George is a lazy piece of shit."

Gretta's belligerent tone squeezed the patience from my body.

"Have you considered divorce?"

"Your first solution is to end the marriage? You're some psychologist."

My body stiffened. "That question was to discern how dismayed you are by the situation, not a recommendation."

"A divorce is exactly what I want to get rid of mush man."

"Why haven't you filed?"

"Because I'd be the villain, the bad one. Everyone thinks he's a saint. The kids would side with him—blame me. They don't understand that I need a real man, not a fluff wad. A real man doesn't run every time his mom whines. A man who'll take me in bed like a warrior is what I deserve."

"You want the divorce to be his fault?"

"Duh, I don't want blamed. I need justification for taking the house and savings. A reason that'll convince my kids he deserved to be left with nothing."

"Perhaps you two could come to an agreement—half everything. Tell everyone it's a mutual decision to end your marriage."

"Then he wins."

"He wins?"

"Have you not heard a word I've said, Marcy? I deserve everything for putting up with him. He's ruined my life."

My words came out mechanical and firm. "Here's my advice, Gretta. File for divorce and accept the aftermath." I stood.

Her eyes squinted. "You can help."

"What are you talking about?" I slowly lowered into my chair.

"I left Theo's company. I'm Celeste's secretary now. She told me that you know a whore who can seduce my husband. If George cheats I'll threaten to divorce him for adultery. He'd be so embarrassed I'd get anything and everything I wanted."

I felt fire rise from my chest. Gretta didn't seem to notice the flesh I felt reddening on my cheeks and neck. "I'll take care of George," I said through tight lips. "Pay Von, in cash, on your way out."

I heard Von and her squabbling.

"You people always want money first," she yelped. "A hundred bucks for a chat with an old friend. You're out of your mind."

"Pay up," his acidic tone could've melted money.

"Well, I never."

I stood in the doorway. "Pay or your services end here. Also, five hundred cash is required before I arrange your solution."

"I don't carry that much money," she whooped.

"Get the money here before 5 p.m. or the plan is terminated."

Her sneer reflected mine as she dug five one-hundred-dollar bills from her purse. "Want my heart, too?"

I thought about pointing out she didn't have one, but didn't.

She tried to slam the door, but it closed automatically. Nothing left to vent her anger but to stomp her feet.

Von stood and straightened his jacket. "What's her deal?"

"Wants her husband trapped."

"You're willing to help that witch?"

"In a manner of speaking." I smiled.

Von reciprocated, "Interesting."

My feet drug as I returned to my desk. I pushed in Barbee's number.

"You up for another job?"

"Is it that crazy guy?"

"No."

"Sure, I'll take it."

"Eastside Motel and Diner at 6 p.m."

"Do I need to wear my secretary outfit? My hair is rainbow again."

"Yes on the clothes. Don't worry about your hair color."

As soon as I hung up, I punched in Celeste's number, thinking my anger had subsided enough to be rational.

"What's up, girl?" Her tone uncharacteristically happy, "Calling to divulge the truth about my husband?"

"Gretta was here. Why did you rat me out to that woman?"

"Tired of her griping about her old man. He needs dumped and you can help. Be a special service to my psyche."

"By the way, Celeste, Deke screwed Barbee hard and long. Have a good day." *Wasn't my day to be rational after all.*

The phone quivered in my hand as I pushed the off button. It started buzzing seconds later. I found the word mute and pushed.

———— ◆ ————

Eastside was nothing like the upscale hotels that Celeste and her wealthy friends had selected for their husbands.

George came through the diner door twenty minutes early. He sat in a corner booth. He gulped the first beer, then gently sipped the second. He fingered a napkin, then wadded and threw it across the table. Quickly recovering it, he looked toward the bartender as if afraid he'd be caught vandalizing. Placing a new napkin opposite him he flattened it, then pinched his cheek as he looked toward the door.

Barbee entered with a flurry. Green and red hair celebrated the Christmas season. Her conservative black suit seemed out of place. Apparently, she'd sold or misplaced the black heels I bought. Gold sparkly slippers adorned her feet. She was a fashion wreck that didn't look too out of place in a cheap motel.

She hopped onto a stool two down from me. I nodded toward the man in the booth. Her right foot touched the floor.

"Not yet," I hissed, and touched my watch.

Her tongue poked out.

I didn't plan to trap George, but I was curious if he'd take the Barbee bait. Good to know what kind of man I was supporting.

Five minutes later George's side of the conversation echoed in the near empty bar. "Okay, sorry that you're sick. I'll hurry home."

I tapped the bar to stray Barbee's attention from a biker guy then tilted my head in George's direction. He was in the process of leaving.

The stool scraped as Barbee pushed back and speed-walked toward him.

"Geez, you look familiar. Where do I know you from?"

George lifted a napkin and absorbed the sweat beads that formed across his forehead. "Don't know, miss."

"It's George, right?"

His head startled back, "Well, yes, but sorry to say I don't recollect who you are?"

"Barbee."

"I best get home."

Barbee laughed, "I forbid it! Not until we figure out where I met you."

She slid into the booth. His legs maneuvered back under his side of the table.

Hand it to Barbee, she certainly knew how to improvise.

A waitress appeared at the table. "You two ready to order?"

"I'm starved," Barbee said. "Fried chicken for me. You want the same, George?"

He shook his head.

George reminded me of that long-eared dog a neighbor had when I was a kid. Owner used to kick him in the belly every time he barked. After two weeks the poor thing dropped dead. After a few more years with Gretta, George would likely have done the same.

I heard every word, mostly Barbee, while I slowly sipped beer. She reviewed all the way back to elementary school trying to find the nonexistent time when she and George met.

"I'm thinking it must've been a one-night stand, George. Maybe we were too drunk to remember."

His face took on the hue of an overripe tomato. "I would've remembered you." His words so muffled I barely caught them.

"Oh, how sweet," Barbee gushed. "I have a motel room.

We could have sex that'll refresh our memories."

"I couldn't," he whispered.

"Please, George, I really like you."

"No, no, no," he knocked against the table edge, when he stumbled to stand.

I hurried toward him. "Please wait."

George startled, a deer about to bolt into the forest.

"Sit, please."

Slowly he moved back into the booth, while I pushed beside Barbee.

"Here's the deal, George. Can you keep a secret?"

"I can," he stuttered.

"Gretta hired us. She wanted you to cheat so she could blame you for a divorce. She's after all the money, possessions, and support from your children."

Paleness crept into his complexion. "Oh?"

"Does this surprise you?" I queried.

"Not really. Sounds like something she'd concoct to hurt me."

I continued, "How do you feel about Gretta?"

"Meanest person I ever knew."

Barbee piped in. "Why the hell haven't you left her?"

"To stay with my children. She'd never have allowed me to see them. I was a buffer against her evil tongue and actions."

"They're grown now?" I questioned, but already knew.

"Yes, both in college. Won't be able to give them financial support if I'm broke."

"George, tell me what to do. Do I tell her you made passionate love to a stranger, or that you were faithful?"

George pinched at his cheek. "Don't know."

"Let's talk it through. If I tell her you were faithful she'll still be your wife. On a personal note, she'll continue hounding me to trap you. If we tell her you cheated, she'll file for divorce, and claim adultery, which she can't prove."

"You'd tell her I made love to Barbee?"

"Not by name, but I'll tell her you made love to a stranger."

"She'd never expect I'd have the balls."

My blunt words came out before I considered stifling them. "That's a logical conclusion since she doesn't think you have balls at all."

George didn't seem offended.

"You can ask her for a divorce," I offered. "My concern is she'll take everything. Claim desertion or some other stupid thing."

George spoke slowly, "I can pull half of our assets to a separate account."

Glad that his mind moved quickly from shock to action, "That might work."

His body rocked forward as he shook his head in the affirmative. "I'll start the process tomorrow."

I reassured him, "You'll know you didn't commit adultery, and your children will believe you. You can even volunteer to take a lie detector test."

George summarized, "I'll be embarrassed, but rid of her."

"Exactly," my word sang out.

His next words blunt and certain, "Tell her I had sex with a stranger—hot, turbulent sex with me on top."

"I'll do it, George. Please keep Barbee and me out of this."

"You're my saviors, and I'll protect you," he promised.

Barbee winked at George. "Goodbye. I bet you'll remember me next time."

"Forever, Barbee, forever."

His body stood straight as he exited the bar.

Barbee grinned, "Seemed like a teddy bear. Too bad I didn't get to teach him a couple of hot sex moves with him on top."

"Think of this as another sort of good deed. We're screwing his wife, which is a very special orgasm."

"Listen to that dirty mouth of yours. I always thought you had some spit." Barbee fist-bumped my shoulder.

"More than you'll ever know my friend."

———◆———

My bed beckoned when I arrived home. However, worry mixed with jubilation kept my brain in high gear. If this went wrong I could lose my license. There wasn't any proof. An all cash deal—no motel room rented. Three friends talked in a café booth. The male of the group left alone.

The phone buzzed four times during the night and three times early next morning. I imagined Gretta slipping into a closet, or riding her broom outside, in order to get out of George's hearing range.

A couple of weeks would give him time to stash half their assets. Eventually, I'll phone her. How should I begin the conversation? "George really does have balls, and he knows how to work a real woman." That would work.

CHAPTER TWENTY-NINE

MURDER AGAIN

I was looking forward to a restful Saturday, because I had no shelter clients scheduled that day. I sat at my breakfast bar, and unrolled the newspaper. A woman's face stared at me, the words FOURTH MURDER stretched above her photo. Hot liquid drizzled down my chin and onto the collar of my pink nightshirt.

The story reported that Jenny Adams, age 19, was found dead in a motel room. The police suspected that the same person who killed Jenny had murdered three other prostitutes.

Jenny's face was everywhere. I saw her in my second cup of coffee as I poured creamer. In the clouds when I looked out the window. Her eyes returned my expression when I glanced in the mirror.

"I know, Jenny, you'd be alive if I hadn't screwed up the search. It's my fault you're dead."

A throw pillow absorbed my tears but nothing took the ache out of my chest or her young face out of my brain.

My hand trembled as I pushed in Zane's number, then Earl, and lastly, Samuel's. They each got the same request: Come to my apartment at noon for pizza and a plan.

I pulled on a black sweatshirt and gray jogging pants. Slicked my hair into a ponytail. I cleaned the bathroom and then vacuumed the apartment. Anything to keep my body moving and my mind occupied.

By twelve-fifteen the three men munched pizza and sipped beer in my living room.

"What's up?" Samuel asked then took another bite of pizza.

I couldn't help but smile. "Maybe I wanted my three favorite men over for lunch."

Zane's usual look of suspicion focused on me. "I'm sure you've never used my name and favorite in the same sentence before."

"That's true," I agreed.

Earl shook his head. "No offense, but you look like crap. What've you been crying about?"

I unfolded the newspaper, and held it in front of my chest. "Jenny Adams is dead because I screwed up the search of Matthew's house."

Samuel's words heaved. "A lunatic killed her."

My tears made slow paths down my cheeks. "I gave him the opportunity."

Zane's intense stare confronted me. "Tears won't bring her back."

I managed to meet his eyes. "I'll feel guilty for the rest of my life if I don't help catch this guy. And I have just the plan to do it."

"And what do you plan to do?" Samuel's fatherly tone irritated me.

"I'm his next prostitute."

"No way," Earl's voice spiked. "You have no business playing undercover agent."

Zane jumped in, "No background, no experience, you'd get yourself killed."

"Thanks for your cynicism—jerk."

"I agree with them," Samuel's voice calm, patronizing. "You need to stay out of this."

"Here's the deal, guys. I'm doing this with or without you. If you won't help me I'll find a couple of FRIENDS who will."

"Damn it!" Zane's fork stabbed a pizza slice.

Contemptuous words flooded from my lips. "Thought

chances of getting evidence and catching the guy would multiply with a cop, detective, and a tough guy at my back. Since that's not happening—get out. I have calls to make."

Zane stood. "You stubborn little wench. Won't listen to reason."

Earl and Samuel didn't move as Zane headed toward the door.

Zane's words stung. "Let's get out of here, guys. Don't let her manipulate you."

"She means it," Samuel said. "It's us or some rookies she picks up."

"I'm in," Earl announced.

Zane's jaw dropped. "Damn it guys. She's got you both whipped."

"LEAVE," I ordered.

"I'd be fired for letting a civilian do undercover work."

"Then get out!"

Zane's anger leached out as he tromped toward the door. "Regardless, I'd never play the third bitch in your trio."

A few seconds of silence as the door slammed behind him. A gargle of laughter erupted form Earl's mouth, setting off Samuel.

"Me with male bitches, life is good."

"Let's get our plan worked out," Samuel advised.

———————◆———————

For the second Friday night in a row I stood on this street corner, boobs overflowing in a red knit top, black mini skirt, and thigh-high boots. A tattoo shop on the corner and four beer joints the only open businesses in this nearly deserted section of town. This was the primary solicitation corner for three of the four dead women. I'd run into a couple of aggressive men. "No" wasn't a word they expected from a working girl. The second time Samuel honked his truck horn to scare a guy off.

The johns had slim whore pickings that night—two older prostitutes and me. Word spread that prostitutes working this particular area ended up on a slab. Another mysterious message leaked out to the girls to take a Friday night break or end up in jail.

It was drizzling tonight, and the moon apparently left with the prostitutes. If he picked one of the whores, I'd butt in loudly. Not likely he'd choose an older woman since the average age of the dead women was twenty-two. He apparently liked to kill the young.

Although I chose to play hooker—to diminish my guilt—standing on a dark street corner was creepy. The first Friday I felt excited but this Friday I'd come to my senses and decided risking my life is nuts. Because I wasn't feeling brave tonight, I hoped Monty wouldn't show.

I hung with the two older women. My eyes constantly surveyed the area. Headlights shown a block up then slowly came toward us. The vehicle pulled up to the curb and stopped beside me. My chest tightened.

Lady on my right mooned him. No panties under her skirt. "Want some of this sweetheart?"

I wandered to get a better look at the driver. Monty's eyes met mine. Good thing the darkness kept him from seeing my terror.

"You," his finger motioned.

My competition didn't give up. "Come on baby I can do things that little skank doesn't know exists."

Monty's words were enough to burn, "GET LOST."

The prostitute pointed a finger. "You're goin' pay, new girl."

That's what I feared—paying big time. I maneuvered past her and into Monty's passenger seat.

"Where to?" he said.

I kept my voice low, attempting to control the tremble. "Siren's Motel, four blocks east."

"I know it."

Silence filled the car. Should've asked Barbee what was polite whore conversation while being transported to and from raunchy sex.

"Lousy weather," I said.

"Shut up," he responded.

So I did.

Five minutes later he spoke. "Room number?"

"37."

"Go. Get naked. I'll follow in ten."

My hand shook the card into the door slot. It didn't open.

I pushed again. Nothing. Sweat dripped down my sides. I examined the card. Wrong side, tried again, door clicked. I turned on one side lamp.

"Earl needs more light," Samuel directed through my bug.

I switched on the bathroom light, and left the door open. Tugged off my boots, pulled my red top over my head and quickly removed the skirt. I rushed for cover, knowing that Earl watched every move from a monitor.

Minutes later the door opened. Monty hovered at the end of the bed. "PULL DOWN THAT COVER. SPREAD YOUR LEGS."

"I want you, mmm-man. Got some sweet stuff for you, mister."

His mouth curved, "You're an evil woman."

"Take off your pants. Be bad with me," I spouted.

His body straightened. Words boomed, "NO WOMAN TELLS ME WHAT TO DO, ESPECIALLY NOT SCUM."

"Please man, show me what you got. You know you want some. I got it for you. Aren't you a real man?"

"I give the orders here. SHUT YOUR FILTHY MOUTH."

"I know where I'd like to shut it," I whispered.

"NO, JEZEBEL."

"Come on mister, quit playing, show me what you got. Or maybe you got nothing worth seeing."

He circled to the side of the bed. He whispered, "I do have something for you." He cupped my cheeks. You'll feel the heat tonight."

"Make me burn."

His hands circled my neck. Light pressure then he yelled, "HELL FIRE."

He squeezed harder. The room went dark. Only a single flicker left in my murky brain.

Earl's voice ordered Monty to stop. A chair crashed as Earl threw him toward the wall.

I heard the clamp of handcuffs and Samuel's voice, "The cops are on the way, asshole."

Earl pulled the sheet over my naked body. "Say something, Marcy."

"I'm okay," I whimpered.

Minutes later I heard Zane's voice through the fog in my

head. He was reading Monty his rights. He must have been patrolling the neighborhood. Perhaps looking out for me. *He'd never admit that.*

"I'm taking you to the emergency room to make sure you're okay," Earl said.

"I'm fine, take me home."

Zane broke in, "Earl, call an ambulance. We'll interview her later."

"I want to go home."

"This isn't about what you want. Case needs medical verification of the assault."

"Oh, I get it."

"About time you got something," Zane grunted. "Less oxygen to your brain is scary."

"Let up," Earl reprimanded.

Zane's lip curled as his eyes shot daggers toward Earl.

———— ♦ ————

Four hours later I crawled into my own bed. Von and Earl stood in the doorway.

"Can you stay home tonight, Von?" Earl asked.

"Planned to."

"Good, better if she's not alone."

"Von, please bring a glass of water."

"Sure."

Earl sat at the edge of the bed. "You're a damn good actress lady. I believed that prostitute."

"I pretended he was you." *Oops, where did that come from? Must have taken too many pain pills.*

Earl stood. "Well, time to go."

Oh no, my dirty mouth freaked him out.

"Need to pick up three or four bags of ice to get my temperature, among other things, down."

He gently kissed me on the forehead.

I touched my lips. "You didn't notice, but I do have lips under my nose."

"Goodnight, Marcy," he said with a weary smile, then went out the door.

"Was I gone long enough?" Von inquired when he handed

me the water.

"Too long considering I made a fool of myself. I'll blame it on the drugs and lack of oxygen."

Von crawled into bed. "What's going on in your brain, Marcy?"

"Confusion. I feel a connection with Earl, but I have this love/hate thing with Zane. I thought it might end up as love, but mostly I'm turned off because he's obnoxious."

"Remember your interest in Deke the unobtainable? Maybe you have a fetish for going after what's hard or impossible to get. Want to control men, whether it's good for you or not. Anyway, Zane isn't your type."

"Brutal honesty, hey. Remember I was choked tonight."

"Don't play that choked card with me—you lived."

Our laughter blended.

"True confessions time," Von stammered. "I'm no different from you. I've been embarrassed to tell you, but I started seeing an ashamed gay."

"Oh no, Von. That's not what you deserve."

"I'm his boy on the side and that's all I'll ever be. Wanted to find the love of my life someday and get married. Now I'm involved with a guy who is embarrassed to be seen with me."

"You love him?"

"Not certain."

"Worth giving up the search for your husband-to-be? The children you want to adopt? Are you willing to return to the closet and hide for the guy?"

He didn't hesitate. "No, I'm not."

"What are you going to do about it?"

"Text him."

"Sounds a bit brutal."

"He's always cancelling our dates by text. Sends messages to stay in the restroom if someone he knows walks in while I'm away from our dining table."

"No offense, but it doesn't really sound like he loves you," I ventured.

"I'm lonely, I guess. Tired of waiting for the right one, so I settled."

He pulled the phone out of his pocket and read aloud as he texted. "Going my separate way. Want a future with a man who's not afraid to be gay. I wish you the best. Goodbye."

"I'm impressed, Von, you made a decision to move on. Now it's done."

"Proud of myself, but sad." Suddenly his tone changed. "Tomorrow I start my search for Mr. Wonderful."

"Falling asleep," I murmured. "Sorry."

"Yep, I see those heavy eyelids. I'll watch television for a while. Holler if you need anything."

The nightmare woke me once during the night. I shot to an upright position my breathing labored, my body sweat drenched.

Von wrapped his arms around me. "It's okay, sister—a bad dream—shush."

His arms remained. My eyes closed.

CHAPTER THIRTY

SHE-DEVILS A PHONE CALL AWAY

When I pulled on my brown slacks and striped sweater Friday morning after spending most of the workweek at home I felt only one certainty—I still didn't feel like seeing clients. Emotional and physical tiredness were good enough reasons, but the mass of red and blue bruises circling my neck would require explanation to clients. As soon as I walked in the office door, I asked Von to cancel my appointments. After which he placed a paperwork pile on my desk.

"For you, boss lady. Couple of these reports are due Monday."

"Yes, your majesty."

He reached a handful of small white forms toward me. "Here are your phone messages. Including eight each from your two favorite women, Gretta and Celeste. They've both gone ballistic. I told them you were sick and not to bother you. They don't voice any sympathy."

"Damn. Probably a good morning to call since I don't have enough energy to explode."

"Think of the return calls as a gift to Secretary Von. Hearing their hateful voices in my ear one more time may result in a prison term for strangling the pair. Every time one of their names shows on the caller ID I have a sharp pain in my ass."

"I'll do it for you, although I'd rather slaughter a pig at midnight."

"Some similarities I'm sure," Von giggled as he left.

My smile disappeared. Perhaps this wasn't a good day. *Get it done, coward.* They couldn't kill me over the phone and I can't see their belligerent faces. Better to call before one or both of them show up at the office or home.

Celeste answered on the first note.

Her sharp tone assaulted my ear. "About time you called back. I don't appreciate your rudeness."

"You aren't my top priority, Celeste. You may be amazed to know you didn't make the top one hundred or even thousand for that matter."

"How cute."

"What do you want, Celeste?"

"Deke claimed that he didn't screw your little whore. Before I file for divorce I want the truth."

My internal anger gage rose. "What about that shit you fed me at the restaurant when you badgered me into your sex experiment? Remember you didn't care whether Deke cheated. You promised no one's marriage would be ruined."

"I didn't think he'd cheat on ME!"

"Now you're considering dumping Deke. The best thing about you is your husband. Here's the truth: he didn't cheat, he didn't sway—solid in his commitment to you."

"You almost destroyed my marriage. Why did you lie?"

"You betrayed my trust and sicked Gretta on me. Not to mention putting me in the position of emotionally and financially damaging George, a good man. You deserved to get what you dealt out—PAIN."

"I'll get your counseling license revoked," she threatened.

"Go for it! You were never my client, nor was Gretta. There wasn't a confidentiality requirement. On the other hand, I was your client in graduate school. You breached confidentiality when you told Gretta about my unconventional work with women. So, DEAR, I might get scorched, but you'll get burned if there's a battle."

I heard an object slammed against something, then the phone went dead. Apparently, Celeste attacked her cell phone.

I poked the off button. Never again did I intend to hear Celeste's venomous voice.

Before I backed out, my fingers quickly punched in Gretta's number.

"I have several messages from you, Gretta."

"That's because you're too high and mighty to return calls. You've left me at a standstill."

I inserted a bit of pity in my tone. "Just uncomfortable telling you the truth. George took the bait. He topped the prostitute and gave her a fine ride. She didn't even want paid for the second round."

The line seemed dead. "Gretta, are you there?"

Sulky words seethed into my ear. "George never did that to me."

"There's a clue. If you beat a man down, don't expect him to keep it up."

More silence.

"Congratulations, you now have grounds for divorce!"

"That'll teach the dirty bastard," Gretta raved.

"By the way, I told George you planned to trap him and take all joint possessions and cash. He has everything evenly split by now. You can try to find the man of your dreams, but I think you just lost him forever."

"You filthy witch!"

Glass shattered in the background. If my ears heard correctly I caused my second cell phone destruction this morning.

"It's done." I said as Von's inquiring expression showed up at my desk. "I forgot to ask if you heard from your mystery man."

"Texted, said good while it lasted, and wished me well. So much for him riding in on a white stallion with a gold banner inscribed with—proud to be gay and in love with Von."

"Sorry, my friend. I can tell that you're hurting. But I really think it's for the best."

"I'll survive. I'm going to pick up lunch."

He returned with Chinese thirty minutes later. After lunch I attacked the pile of paperwork.

At 5 p.m. light snow stuck to my hair as I walked to my car. I hoped the snow would keep my Saturday shelter clients home.

CHAPTER THIRTY-ONE

FROZEN HEART

Saturday morning I called Sonya three times hoping for cancellations—no such luck. I drove carefully through the snowy fog on icy streets. At noon I sat at my desk staring at the clock. My one o'clock no-showed, then my two o'clock, no-showed.

The winter storm blew ice prickles against my office window. I paced. I'd hoped for the last hour my 4 p.m. appointment would cancel. If the usual happens the person would no-show, and I'd be thirty minutes later getting home, thus a half-hour deeper into the storm.

A knock barely sounded from the other side of the door. "Come in," I called.

The door swung open. A young face with old eyes peered inquiringly.

"Zoey?"

"Yes," barely squeaked from her lips.

"Come, sit," I directed.

"My friend said you would help me."

"I'll try my best, Zoey."

Her long bangs swept across her face as her head bowed. "I... I... I..." stuttered out.

"Come Zoey, we'll make hot chocolate in the kitchen."

"Okay." she answered, then followed me down the hall.

I pulled out cups. "Check the fridge for whipped topping. Do you like it in your drink?"

"My favorite," she responded.

We carried our drinks back to my office. I pointed for her to sit on one end of the brown tweed sofa. I angled my body into the other end.

She slouched as she sipped the cocoa. A glaze of white foam touched her upper lip.

"How old are you, Zoey?"

"Thirteen."

"You seem more mature than thirteen."

"Granny Nella says I have an old soul."

Nella, the word vibrated my memory. Where have I heard that name?

"I'd like to talk to your old soul. Are you ready? Perhaps then I can begin to understand what broke your spirit."

She licked topping from her lip. "A man—a devil."

"Does your grandma know the man hurt you?"

"No—you can't tell," her voice frantic. "He said he'd fire Granny then tell everyone she's a thief. She'd never cook for anyone again. Papa is sick and I have three brothers. Granny says her job is all that keeps the family alive."

Sweat bubbles formed on my forehead. I remembered Nella—Theo Lisbon's cook. Apprehension caught in my chest, but I kept it from my tone. "Tell me your story, Zoey."

"About a month ago, Mr. Lisbon told me to come upstairs to dust his library shelves. He offered me ten dollars." She paused and took a drink.

"I followed him up the steps. He held the library door open then locked it behind us. His body pressed me against the wall. Called me a pretty little pussy, and said he wanted to pet me. Then his hand brushed down my back. It felt creepy—like bugs crawling inside my body. He turned away, maybe I could've gotten out the door then, but I was afraid. He pulled a pink fuzzy costume out of a drawer, and ordered me to put it on."

Zoey's hand quivered as she downed the rest of her hot chocolate.

"I told him no way would I wear that silly outfit. Guess I sounded hateful because he called me a little bitch and squeezed my face. Told him I didn't have a place to undress."

Zoey's feet moved from the floor to the sofa. She brought her knees up and wrapped her arms around in a fetal position.

"Called me sweetie. Told me nothing I had was new to him. When I said I wouldn't undress he acted nuts. Hissed that he'd fire Granny. Papa would die without his heart medicine because of me."

She stopped a few seconds, her eyes glued on my tear-streaked face.

"I undressed," she continued, "as he watched. I tried to wrap my arms around my naked body. His long stare was scary. Theo threw the costume at me. Called me little pussy, and ordered me to stop crying, and making a fuss. Said I was making big dog biting mad."

Tears swelled in Zoey's eyes. "He stripped in front of me, then put on a spotted dog suit."

Sobs burst out her mouth as she tried to continue her story. My hand squeezed hers, as I waited. Minutes passed before she gained control.

"He pushed his tail into my butt hole, and crammed the thing in and out. I begged him to stop. He leaned over and kissed my back. 'Be a quiet little Zoey kitty, he said. It'll be all right. Big Dog loves his little kitty. Wants to eat her up.' He pulled out his tail and started biting my butt. He stopped when his phone rang. Told me to get dressed, get out, and keep my mouth shut or Granny would pay the consequences for my disobedience. He said I owed Nella for taking my brat brothers, and me when my parents didn't want us. Don't ruin her life, he warned."

The sadness in Zoey's haunted eyes bore into my face. "The next week, I didn't go to work with Granny. She brought me a note from Mr. Lisbon. It said 'need you to finish sorting the books as soon as possible, remember we have a deal.' So that week, and the next, and today…"

"I'm so sorry, Zoey."

"He doesn't wash off me," she whimpered. "No matter how hard I scrub."

"When do you go back to Theo's house?"

"Next week."

"I'll develop a plan. Go home before the weather gets worse. Since you're on Christmas break you'll have to pretend sickness if Theo tells your Granny to bring you."

I walked her to the shelter door. "I promise I'll stop him." Zoey's hug was loose, her demeanor unsure as she left.

That filthy bastard will pay.

———◆———

Von took six rings to answer his cell phone. "What's up, Marcy?"

"Need to talk." I blurted. "Home in fifteen minutes."

"I'll be waiting," he agreed without question.

Twenty minutes later I stood beating my blue sofa back with both fists, as Von watched.

"Marcy, what's going on?"

"Theo's done it again," I huffed.

"His dog sex?"

"With a teenage girl."

"Call the police," Von snarled.

"Teen won't testify. Theo threatened harm to her family. I was too big of coward to have him prosecuted now he's hurting a teenager. But he sure as hell will never hurt a child again. I've got to figure out how to stop Theo without implicating Zoey."

CHAPTER THIRTY-TWO

REVENGE

I swerved my rear toward the floor-length mirror in my bedroom. My long, fuzzy black tail almost touched the floor.

The cat mask covered two-thirds of my face. My chin and eyes the only recognizable features. A scalp net provided the base for the black wig that spoofed curls around my face. The lace body suit emphasized my curves, my legs bare, my heels three inches, and black gloves to keep my prints at bay.

A reason for being at Theo's mansion wasn't difficult to find. A past co-worker spilled that Lisbon was hosting a masked ball on New Year's Eve—a perfect opportunity. Perhaps the spirits were on my side. I pulled the knife from its leather case. I'd sharpened it twenty minutes yesterday, even cut myself as I brushed the sharp blade across a finger. The knife belonged to Dad—thirty-years-old and hard to trace.

The big dog collar was another story. I found it in one of those resale stores with piles of worn clothes and old books. I bought it and a rusted dog pan. Not likely my purchase would be traced—I think, I hope. I pushed the collar, kitty mask, flats and knife into my bag, slipped on a coat to cover my outfit and headed out the door.

Going alone was risky. However, I didn't want witnesses, or anyone I care about being charged as an accessory if I were caught.

I pushed the plan out of my mind, as I drove. Why was I not shaking? Not afraid? A dull ache in my head and the clinch of my hands on the steering wheel indicated a little internal tension. The eyes that met my fixed stare in the rear view mirror conveyed nothing but resolve... and anger. An evil grin stretched my lips. Maybe I'd find new friends in prison.

At almost midnight, as planned, I parked my Camry two blocks from Theo's mansion. Expensive cars lined the curved driveway. Music blasted from the house. Slowly I walked up the sidewalk waiting for someone to leave so my entry didn't require ringing the bell and a greeter. A pair of partygoers, dressed like monkeys, exited the front door, which gave me the opportunity to slip in.

No one even glanced up, and Theo was too engaged with a white sexy bear to notice a new guest. He constantly petted her butt as they stood in front of his aquarium.

"Grrr," she growled, as he nuzzled her neck.

A sexy bear hanging on Theo was a problem. The pair in heat could mean a long wait for me to carry out my plan.

"Almost midnight," Theo bellowed across the crowd.

"Auld Lang Syne" sprang from the intercom system as animals yipped, growled, kissed, and toasted the New Year.

Theo stood and raised a glass, "Glad to begin the year with you animals, but leave before you turn back into people. Not a sight I care to see."

There was a little nervous laughter but it wasn't long before they took Theo's blatant hint. Coats retrieved, thank you and goodbyes called out, and the crowd almost gone. I snuck into the kitchen. Lights dim, a pot of coffee perking for sobering up drunks, and stacked dishes. Apparently Nella finished her tasks before going home.

The pantry offered respite. There I'd stay as the rest of the partygoers thinned out.

A few minutes later it was quiet. I ventured back into the kitchen, opened the door a couple of inches and listened.

White Bear invited from the sofa. "Want it here, Big Dog?"

Theo's drunken bark rang out.

Vomit gurgled in my throat.

A playful voice teased, "Wrestle me, dog."

"Don't talk," he ordered.

"Big Dog must be rabid. You're a grouch."

"SHUT UP."

"Grrr," Bear growled.

"Go home," Theo ordered. "You ruined the mood."

"I'm too liquored up to drive," Bear protested.

"GET OUT."

His penetrating yell sunk into my head and propelled my heart into a rapid thump.

"BASTARD," she screeched, then a minute later "bastard, bastard, bastard" rang out as her voice got further away.

The front door slammed. I grabbed a bowl from the counter, and smashed it onto the floor into a hundred pieces.

"What the hell?" Theo's voice bellowed from outside the kitchen.

The spotted dog stopped in the doorway and stared at me, Black Kitty, leaning against his refrigerator. "What are you doing in my kitchen, pretty kitty?"

"Meow," I said, then turned pulling my tail to the side to expose my bare butt.

"What's your name sexy kitty?"

"Meow," my only reply. I tugged him to a chair, then clamped the dog collar around his neck.

"Me-you, me-you," I purred, pulling at the leash until he came down on his hands and knees. I led him around the room.

"Now kitty," he begged.

"Doggie needs bath," I whispered.

Theo leaned against the wall with legs spread eagle.

I clamped the leash end to a door handle and turned toward the sink.

"Hurry, kitty!"

"Shut your eyes for a surprise," my words thick with promise.

A mist of steam rose from the boiling coffee as it poured onto Theo's genitalia. His eyes bugged as if possessed. A roar pierced from his mouth for just a second then his head sank toward the floor. His tethering to the doorknob halted the total collapse of his body.

I watched his body roll sideways. His face smashed into the tile floor, as I retrieved the leash and collar. One last time, I glanced back to view the pile of dog shit on the kitchen floor.

CHAPTER THIRTY-THREE

SUSPECT

Insanity—my self-diagnosis for scheduling a New Year's Day football watching party. At the time it seemed like a way to look innocent, not to mention bring back some normalcy to my life. Now I felt drained, exhausted from the demise of Theo.

No television reports, no newspaper or Internet news for me that day. I didn't know if Theo was alive or dead. Wasn't even sure if it was possible to murder a man by boiling his private parts. Surely, it at least disarmed him.

The coffee was a gift, a sudden decision. At the time, seemed like the best choice, better than blood splatter that might have landed on me. Perhaps not as good as killing him, but if his penis was dead, my goal was accomplished.

Sorry—no. Frightened—yes. Criminals think they've accomplished perfect crimes, but they always make a mistake. One flaw could send me to prison. My brain kept hammering on what mistake I'd made. I never took the gloves off. Didn't touch Theo's clothes or body. A net and a wig covered my hair. I arrived with the New Year so no one paid any attention to me. The perfect crime? No such thing I'd heard Samuel say.

The white bear was my only worry. She was the last animal seen with Theo, the logical perpetrator. If she was arrested, what would I do? No way could I have planned for all those people to see Theo and the bear left alone right before his tragic loss.

So I'd found the flaw. Bear being wrongly accused would equal my confession. Damn Theo to hell. He might get revenge, even if he was dead.

A voice shouted from outside my apartment, "Open the door, Marcy."

I flung it open to let in Von, three pizzas, and one carton of ice cream.

"Geez, Marcy, you look like shit."

He pushed the ice cream container into the freezer as I spread the pizza boxes across the breakfast bar.

He turned and studied my face. "What've you been up to?"

"Don't be so suspicious and insulting," I sneered.

"Theo?"

My legs turned to mush. I grabbed a stool for support. "Why are you bringing him up?"

"On the news."

"Tell me," I squeaked.

"Someone attacked him last night or early this morning. Local television report kept some of the information confidential. Internet let it all hang out."

My word croaked out, "Dead?"

"No, in fair condition, badly burned. No future rapes for him."

"That's good to know."

Von's tone softened. "Why didn't you let me help?"

"My fight."

"Come with me." He took my hand and pulled toward the bedroom.

"Sit on the end of the bed while I get the supplies."

"Supplies?"

"I'm going to put some color in your face. Nothing says guilty like pale lips and red, blotchy skin. No way to look at your own party."

I sat statue still as Von's hand deftly brushed light rose on my cheeks, pale blue on my eyelids, and pink on my lips

He studied his handiwork, "Much better."

Next he whipped out the curling iron and tamed my wayward hair.

"Do I look innocent yet?"

"Almost, take off that sloppy sweatshirt." I watched as his hand picked through my closet. A pink sweater and blue jeans landed on my bed.

"Suit up and cheer up girl, while I put out the drink glasses."

My transformation complete, I glanced in the mirror. A butterfly had emerged from a dark cocoon. A new page for the criminal's handbook—look innocent in pink. Unfortunately, my brain was still in a dark dungeon of "what ifs."

Over the next thirty minutes I played hostess greeting Earl and Sonya. Samuel was spending the day with Eva's family. Maybelle was supervising the shelter.

Company chatter allowed me to remain quiet except for an occasional "yes."

"Where's Zane?" Von asked.

Sonya responded, "Working that Theo Lisbon burning. The world is a cruel place. How do people inflict such pain on others?"

The nut bowl slipped from my hand and crashed to the floor—a deluge of glass fragments and peanuts.

Von's words rang out. "How many beers did you have before we showed up?"

My voice quivered. "Sorry, did the glass hit anyone?"

Earl quipped. "You'll have to aim a little better if you want a casualty."

Von laughed, "Those peanut attacks are devastating."

I retrieved the broom and dustpan from the closet and absorbed a few tears into my sweater sleeve.

My broom was hard at work sweeping up glass and nuts when Zane arrived. A quick "hi" in his direction, then I searched for pieces of glass under the counter, and in front of the fridge. Bright little particles of sharpness hid from my broom. Searching, searching, trying to never look into Zane's eyes.

"That's enough, Marcy," Zane's voice a rough whisper from the other side of the breakfast bar. "Let's talk."

"Can't it wait? I'm having a party."

"No. It's official business." Zane's voice rose louder. His features hardened.

Von looked up from the television. "Come on, Zane, take a break. It's lunch time."

"I'm on duty," Zane retorted.

Earl moved toward Zane. "What's Marcy's connection to your case?"

Zane ignored him.

"Marcy, do you want to be questioned alone?"

"I'd prefer you attacked me in front of witnesses."

"Fine with me."

The sports announcers verbally sparred in the background, my visitors quiet.

Zane stood on one side of the bar, me on the other. My spoon swirled round and round dissolving the sweetener in my coffee.

"I feel like a mouse under a cat's paw." A nervous laugh escaped my mouth.

Zane's attack started. "Theo Lisbon—the guy who suffered the tragic loss of his cock early this morning. You know him, right? Fired you a few years back?"

"Actually, his underling fired me. Theo didn't do menial tasks."

"Perhaps you had a score to settle?" Zane used his calm policeman voice, the one to make a person think it was safe to share information.

I stood, silent. Where was this going? He couldn't know... unless he followed me.

"Interesting smell in Theo's kitchen," Zane continued. "You know how you mix those two perfumes together to get the scent you like?"

I didn't answer.

"When I was standing in Theo's kitchen you popped into my mind. Took awhile, but then I realized why. I smelled the combined scents—I smelled you."

"Surprised you're into women's fragrances," I scoffed.

"Little later a woman called me. She said Marcy Simon should be investigated, because you hated Theo. I talked to half a dozen people you used to work with who agreed you

186

had a score to settle. Said he used you for sex then had you fired the next day. Any of this wrong?"

"Your primary witness is someone who hates me?"

"Main report was from the parking lot security guard. He said you rammed the back of Mr. Lisbon's car. Said he saw the bruises and bites Theo inflicted on you. Told me Lisbon deserved what he got. My main contact sympathized with you. Isn't that a strange coincidence?"

"Actually, Theo helped me. If he hadn't fired me I never would've gotten an education. Not logical that I'd risk my good life for something that happened years ago."

"That's the part I haven't figured out. Why would you?"

Von's voice chimed in, "Internet said party goers reported that Theo was with his lover when they left."

"Lisbon said he and the woman quarreled and he ordered her out."

"Maybe she came back," Sonya stated.

"Lisbon said someone else attacked. Beautiful, with blue eyes that put him in a trance, and he admitted being drunk. Where were you between midnight and 2 a.m., Marcy?"

"At home."

Zane's tone raspy, "You're lying."

Von piped in, "With me," then pointed at the sofa. His finger moved, "Watching that television. How dare you call Marcy a liar? Your entire life is a lie. Being mean doesn't make you more masculine, or any less gay. Be who you are."

Sonya's mouth gaped.

Zane's face turned red then faded to white. "You son-of-a-bitch, I trusted you."

"Marcy's my friend. I won't let you beat on her. Get out."

Anger shook Zane's deflated body as he stormed out the door.

"I never even suspected," were Sonya's last words before grabbing her purse and running out the door after her son.

I turned to Von. "Why didn't you tell me about your relationship with Zane?"

"I promised to keep it secret."

"But now you told—for me?"

"Of course, better to betray your lover, than your best friend."

I pressed my tear-stained face against his. "You're the best BFF in the universe. I can never repay you."

He kissed me square on the lips. "Remember how you searched for me—you saved my life. We'll call it even."

"Everyone on the sofa," Earl ordered. "Should calm us to watch grown men tackle each other while people holler."

"That does sounds tranquil compared to Marcy's party," Von agreed.

Von and I snuggled at one end of the sofa. Earl sat at the other end, his hand resting on the cushion. I lay my hand over his.

An hour later Von stretched and rose. "Enough football until next year. Got a headache with a little heartache. Going to bed."

I followed him to the door, and wrapped my arms around him. "I'm sorry you got tangled in my mess."

"Where I chose to be."

"Are you okay about Zane?"

"Mark it up to one more man who wouldn't come out of the closet for me. Goodnight."

"Come here," Earl gestured then pulled me beside him on the sofa. "I keep asking myself why you'd burn a guy's junk."

"Perhaps because he raped a thirteen-year-old girl multiple times. Maybe he threatened to fire, and discredit her grandmother if the teen told the truth. Perhaps this child had no escape that would keep her anonymous. Could be I promised her Theo the devil would never hurt her again. I owed her that much."

"You owed her?"

"Theo raped me a few years back. If I'd reported him Zoey might never have gone through this trauma."

Earl's expression remained flat.

I looked out the picture window. "I'm a damaged woman."

"You aren't damaged."

"I feel like I am. Theo intertwined sex with violence, now it seems wrong to enjoy something that left such grief."

His hand squeezed mine. "There's a big difference between sex with love, and violent sex."

"I'm afraid I'll never beat my demons. That's not fair to any man."

"I'd like to help you destroy them. That's if you think you could ever learn to love a man who's scarred and ugly. We're the real life version of beauty and the beast."

"You're confused about something."

His eyes widened, "What's that?"

"You're the beauty. I'm the beast."

THE END

MORE BY THIS AUTHOR

Sheriff Lexie Wolfe Novels

Killing the Secret

Somebody is murdering the women who played on a championship basketball team twenty years ago. Sheriff Lexie searches for the link between the women that provoked someone to want them all dead.

Deadly Search

Sheriff Lexie becomes entangled in a web of deceit as she searches for her father's murderer. Her temptress mother may be the reason her father was killed.

Terror's Grip

Lexie's right arm suspended above her held by a chain attached to a two-inch metal clamp around her wrist. Her left hand fisted and punched forward as if a boxing bag or her captor's new face dangled in front of her. Her scream filled the cold darkness. "I WON'T DIE WEAK!"

Murder & Beyond

Sheriff Lexie and Deputy Tye Wolfe are enmeshed in the strangest cases of their law enforcement careers. Two teenage girls vanish. Tye doesn't believe that Wendy is a witch. Lexie doesn't think the ocean swallowed Emma.

Deranged Justice

Local citizens panic when Sheriff Lexie doesn't solve a series of bizarre murder cases. An irrationally jealous woman and man who demands custody of her adopted nephew add more turmoil to her life.

Anthologies

"Come Die with Me" in *A River of Stories*

"Old Guys and Dead People" in *Shades of Tulsa*

An excerpt from *Killing the Secret*, the first Sherriff Lexie Wolfe novel:

KILLING THE SECRET

Prologue

He decided to stop at a roadside café before he killed her, rather than after. Caffeine after eight p.m. made it difficult for him to sleep and he needed to awake early for his flight. He sure as hell didn't want to oversleep and spend an extra night in Kansas.

As soon as he walked in the café he regretted stopping. The fleeting glances from locals made him feel like a flashing light. The nosy bastards reminded him of the people in Diffee. He was glad he'd put on the wig. It camouflaged a bit of his identity. Smells of grease, smoke, and sweat from people who obviously didn't believe in daily showers assaulted his senses. It felt as if the odors were sticking to his clothes. Nausea roiled in his stomach. He swayed and gripped the edge of the table.

"Are you okay, handsome? I'd be willing to take you home with me for some TLC." The blonde waitress made her offer with a crooked smile.

"I want coffee with cream," he ordered as he turned and stared out the window. He needed to remember why he was in this disgusting place, maybe then his resolve could override the sick feeling. All seven must die. Tonight Tina will be the second.

Terri, the first, was hardly worth his time. She was dying of cancer but he knew she must die in his time frame—not God's. Being Catholic might motivate her to confess her sins on her deathbed and he wasn't about to give her the chance.

The waitress set the cup down with a bang. Brown droplets splashed on the table, barely missing his linen shirt.

"Sorry, handsome," she cooed.

Suppressing the urge to throw the hot coffee in her face, he muttered, "Accidents happen."

She slid her hand softly from his wrist to his elbow.

"Darcy, honey," a man at the bar called out. "Can you quit hittin' on the guy long enough to get me a refill?"

The murderer put a five on the table and left before the white trash returned. He had better things to do.

Chapter 1

Sheriff Lexie Wolfe sat in the small airplane searching below for any sign of life in the Oklahoma backwoods. Most likely their signal would be smoke since it was just above freezing this cold March morning.

Tye and Clay, her deputies, sat across from her. Red, the pilot, tore out the four back seats on the old plane and put in benches so he could hire out for parachute jumping. The interior smelled of cheap liquor—a courage booster left from one of the customers Red had taken up the night before.

The first female sheriff of the small town of Diffee, Lexie had no delusions about why she was elected. Those six years as a cop in Houston and the Masters Degree in Criminology didn't earn the badge on her chest. Sympathy, not experience, had won her the election. Her brother, Tye, traded his right leg for two lives and a Medal of Honor. Her father was brutally murdered and she was left to die when their farmhouse was broken into years before. Those were her vote getters.

The fine features and blue eyes of her Caucasian mother and the skin coloring of her Cherokee father had created a stunning daughter. The illusion of beauty ended up close. Lexie traced the scar down the right side of her face. Her mother raged, cried, and bitched trying to get Lexie to have plastic surgery. Storming back, Lexie told her, "My face is my reminder that Dad's killer is somewhere living a life he doesn't deserve. Every day I touch my scar so my hate won't subside."

"That's sick." Her mother screamed.

Lexie's fingers moved from the scar and started weaving her waist-length black hair into a single braid. She didn't care why she was elected sheriff. All that mattered was the power and facilities she now had to find the person who'd murdered her father. Drug busts usually exhilarated her, but today it seemed like a waste of time. She wanted to be in her office searching records for clues to the murderer instead of jumping out of an airplane.

The hard seat made it impossible for Lexie's butt to find a comfortable position. Seeing her brother, who had to bend and fold himself onto the board seat, sleeping tranquilly across from her was beyond belief.

The Indians won the war of Tye's genes. He showed no physical resemblance to his white mother. His straight black hair was pulled back tightly at the nape of his neck. His skin and eyes were earth shades. Even though he was asleep he exuded strength and a presence.

She felt Red's eyes on her and glanced up to intercept a quick wink. In years past, she'd have gotten angry at his orneriness. Time, however, had healed the rejection she felt from him when she was sixteen. Actually, he had saved her from her own misguided horniness.

Being Tye's best friend, it was common for Red to crash at their house after the guys went out drinking on Friday nights. One morning Tye and her dad left early to go fishing. Mom didn't generally show her face before 10 a.m.

Lexie shed her bathrobe and crawled into bed beside Red, who was sound asleep. She gently smoothed back the red hair from his forehead. Rubbing his chest she caught the hairs between her fingers and made paths across his chest. Ripples of passion possessed her body. Her hand drifted down from his chest to his belly.

Lexie startled when he moved. Red turned to his side and held her. His mouth pressed against hers. Their tongues met for seconds, then he suddenly turned away.

"Go away," he snarled.

Lexie remembered the hatred she felt for months. The rejection and embarrassment were too much for her teenybopper brain. As far as she knew he'd never told anyone about her foiled attempt at seduction.

www.ingramcontent.com/pod-product-compliance
Lightning Source LLC
Chambersburg PA
CBHW031338170626
46807CB00002B/754